"I'm sor[...]
night."

Cole tossed one of her empty creamers in the ashtray. "You didn't give me anything I didn't ask for."

Evie's pale coffee curdled in her mouth. "The best explanation I can come up with is that the confined space of the Conquest, all that time crammed together, created a false air of intimacy."

"False airs," he repeated.

It had been one of her longer opening lines. She dug the hole deeper. "Prolonged closeness can sometimes create weird static electricity between people. Who knows? Maybe it was that stuff they spray in cars to make them smell new."

"Fumes and false airs."

"Right."

He sipped some more.

"You have a better theory?"

"How about lust?"

WHAT ARE *LOVESWEPT* ROMANCES?

They are stories of true romance and touching emotion. We believe those two very important ingredients are constants in our highly sensual and very believable stories in the LOVE-SWEPT line. Our goal is to give you, the reader, stories of consistently high quality that may sometimes make you laugh, sometimes make you cry, but are always fresh and creative and contain many delightful surprises within their pages.

Most romance fans read an enormous number of books. Those they truly love, they keep. Others may be traded with friends and soon forgotten. We hope that each LOVE-SWEPT romance will be a treasure—a "keeper." We will always try to publish

LOVE STORIES YOU'LL NEVER FORGET
BY AUTHORS YOU'LL ALWAYS REMEMBER

The Editors

Loveswept ®769

AMERICAN BACHELORS:

DRIVEN TO DISTRACTION

TERRY LAWRENCE

BANTAM BOOKS
NEW YORK · TORONTO · LONDON · SYDNEY · AUCKLAND

DRIVEN TO DISTRACTION

A Bantam Book / December 1995

If you would be interested in receiving protective vinyl covers for your
Loveswept books, please write to this address for information:

> Loveswept
> Bantam Books
> P.O. Box 985
> Hicksville, NY 11802

ISBN 0-553-44492-1

Published simultaneously in the United States and Canada

Bantam Books are published by Bantam Books, a division of Bantam Dou-
bleday Dell Publishing Group, Inc. Its trademark, consisting of the words
"Bantam Books" and the portrayal of a rooster, is Registered in U.S.
Patent and Trademark Office and in other countries. Marca Registrada.
Bantam Books, 1540 Broadway, New York, New York 10036.

PRINTED IN THE UNITED STATES OF AMERICA

OPM   0 9 8 7 6 5 4 3 2 1

ONE

She'd done it. There was no backing out now. She'd just have to live with the consequences—or die of embarrassment.

A throaty male voice emerged from the car radio. *"You're listening to WRDY, Pine Forest, North Carolina. This is* Austin in the Evening. *Tonight on 'Fiona's Forum,' 'Men Who Can't Commit.' Call us with the name of a man who can't commit and—"*

She'd called. How could she? She glanced at her passenger, his rangy male body barely a foot away in the midsized sedan. If only he'd possessed the conversational skills of a tollbooth collector, a state cop, the computerized voice in the dashboard that told her when she left her lights on, she wouldn't have needed talk radio to fill in the agonizing gaps in their nonexistent dialogue.

"Name your noncommittal male and Fiona Alexander, one of the most talented psychics of this century, will reveal

the location of his destined soul mate. A word of warning, ladies, it might not be you."

"Be careful what you wish for," Fiona said with a chuckle.

She'd had a choice between this or Rush Limbaugh.

Evie gripped the steering wheel and stared grimly at the road. Cole Creek, her seatmate on this car trip from hell, would never know the depths to which she'd sunk. He couldn't. Unless, of course, they announced it live on a nationally syndicated coast-to-coast radio talk show.

Her course was simple. If she heard her voice on the radio, she'd steer for the nearest ditch.

Unfortunately, the flat farmland of Ohio offered few deep ditches. She glared at an exit sign. From their starting point in Dearborn, Michigan, that morning, they'd driven straight south on I-75. After seven hours of freeway and farmland anyone would be bored. Under those circumstances, calling a talk show from a Gas-N-Go sounded almost sensible. A lark. A prank.

"Have I got the man for you," she'd declared when her call was put through from the Gas-N-Go. "He's so noncommittal, he won't give his opinion on the weather."

The producer had laughed then taken her name and a few details about Cole. Evie knew very little about him. He was longtime single. Her friends Bud and Vivian had found setting him up with dates impossible. Not that she'd been fishing. If she'd shown any interest at all, they'd have set *her* up with him. For two years she'd neatly avoided meeting, much less dating, their new mechanic.

Then Bud's back had gone out, preventing him from accompanying her on this trip as planned. That necessitated Cole Creek sitting in. Literally.

She glanced across the car. There he lounged, looking like Sam Shepard, the actor who, in Evie's humble estimation, gave sex appeal its name. Cole's lean face, sinewy body, and craggy all-American features would've given poor Sam a run for his money.

Sky-blue eyes squinted into the semidarkness ahead. A thumb-sized dimple creased his right cheek. His full lower lip was offset by the grim line of the upper one. The man was a walking ad for durable, understated, one-hundred-proof masculinity.

She'd tried for hours to get him to open his mouth. Without input from Cole, she was dangerously likely to jump to her own conclusions. A flicker of an eyelash might mean disapproval. A frown line deepening beside his mouth could be read as stoic endurance or bone-stiffening boredom. Did he think she was too chatty? Too nosy? A total airhead?

He would if he heard her on the radio.

She gripped the wheel harder. She always did this, interpreting men's silences instead of confronting them, anticipating their needs, deciphering opinions instead of asking. Doing all the work in relationships was a major downfall of hers—but up until now she'd only put forth the effort with men she cared about.

She couldn't care about *him.* She hardly knew him. She was driving a brand-new Conquest cross-country to test a highly touted breakthrough in automotive manufacturing and labor management.

As a direct consequence, she faced thousands of

miles trapped in a car with a man she barely knew. When small talk and friendly curiosity proved fruitless, calling a psychic had seemed like a perfectly logical alternative.

It's logic like that that keeps 900 lines in business, Evie thought, shaking her head. As a consumer-magazine writer, she warned people about fraudulent fat-free foods, untrustworthy toasters, sinister siding salesmen. Of all people, she should know better than to call a fortune-teller.

She breathed a sigh of relief when the radio show went to a commercial. For the last hundred miles she'd reassured herself that the program was broadcast live. While she'd dialed, Cole had been outside the Gas-N-Go bending his sleek jeans-clad rear end over the engine. When he'd straightened suddenly and cast a glance her way, she'd hung up fast. They'd had no time to put her on the air.

The commercial ended. *"This is* Austin in the Evening. *Fiona, you were saying during the break that you wanted to talk about a previous caller."*

"Yes, Austin, thank you. I'd like to address my remarks to a woman in Ohio. I sense that you're in transit in your life, my dear. Be assured that the man in question is too. Just remember that life and love aren't destinations. They're but a journey we take together. Perhaps, Eve, your destiny looms closer than you think—"

"Destiny!"

Cole blinked. His head slowly turned. "Pardon me?"

Evie frantically pushed buttons. Heat blasted from the vents, wipers creaked against a dry windshield, a tape ejected, and the clock flashed 12:00. "How do you turn this off?"

"Here." Cole reached over and punched the proper button. Blessed silence filled the car. They drove another four miles. "You were saying?"

She was hoping he'd forgotten. "Uh, how about you? Do you believe in destiny?"

"I'm more interested in our destination."

She bit back a sigh of relief. That left the echo of his low-pitched voice the only sound in the car. She wondered how she'd describe it in a consumer profile? Soft yet gruff, raspy yet smooth. It put her in mind of the cracked leather of an old saddle. The weathered lines of his face were better suited to the great outdoors or the windswept plains than a mechanic's job in a two-man operation on a side street in Dearborn. What was he doing there? Where had he come from? Where were they going?

She snapped back to attention. "Our destination? Here, I'll show you." She twisted around to reach for the maps in the backseat.

Cole reached at the same time. Their arms bumped. "I can get it."

"I'll get it."

"I can get it."

He was stubborn, that much she knew.

Seat-belted in, her knee nudged the underside of the steering wheel while his long legs unfolded on the passenger side. Both of them reached over the split-back bench seat at the same time. They came face-to-face.

The moment stretched like the white lines on the

freeway. Evie glanced at the road, intensely aware of how openly he studied her profile. She hoped the dark hid the heat rushing to her cheeks.

His gaze dropped from her startled eyes to her parted lips. "Let me," he said.

He brought the expandable folder into the front seat. They played a brief tug-of-war for it. Evie won. Settling it on her lap, she pawed through maps of every state in the Union plus the Canadian provinces, ignoring the way her hand trembled. "Oklahoma, no. Iowa, no. New Orleans, not yet. I should alphabetize these."

"Want me to look?"

"I can find it." She squinted in the glow of the control panel at a map of Ohio. "We passed into Kentucky half an hour ago. I was hoping we'd get to Knoxville tonight."

"Why Knoxville?"

"I have reservations." After a day in the car with Cole Creek, she had dozens.

The conversation died away. The miles droned by. She'd hoped talking about their itinerary would give her more to think about than the tanned leather smell of him, the teasing hint of his aftershave, the strong cast of his hands resting on his thighs. Dead wrong, honey. When he turned in his seat she got a whiff of warm male skin, another unhelpful reminder of how close a midsized sedan could be. She'd have to make a note—more passenger room.

"Could you hand me my notepad?"

"Which one?"

"The green one. I think it's in the glove box."

He popped the compartment open. The door

rested on his knee. A small bulb shed light on his lap. He'd slid the seat back the moment he entered the car. She remembered it as if it were minutes earlier instead of hours.

He closed the box with his knee and canted his hips forward in a comfortable slouch. "Here you go."

"Thanks." She flipped the notebook open one-handed. "Drat. This is the one on motels."

"This one?"

"I'm taking notes on service at restaurants, the major hotel chains we'll stay at along the way, security and the single female traveler, and road conditions on our interstate highway system. I have notebooks for each subject to keep my observations straight."

"Except you can't keep the notebooks straight."

"Guess not." She laughed weakly and tossed the notebook in the backseat.

"Checking out gas stations too?"

"Uh, yes." He must have noticed how long she'd been in the Gas-N-Go. Guilt flooded through her. So what if he'd seen her huddling in the phone booth? For all he knew she'd been calling her editor, her parents, Bud and Vivian. In which case why didn't he come right out and ask like any normally curious person?

So she could lie like any normally guilty person.

She took a deep breath. "Even with our late start, we should make Knoxville by midnight. I think we can do without the radio until then, don't you? Uh, Cole, what are you doing?"

A map slid off her lap. Minnesota. Its fold skimmed her thighs like a knife edge. He dropped it in the gaping folder on her lap.

"I can put those away," she said, her voice unaccountably breathy.

"Keep your hands on the wheel, I can do it."

The problem was keeping her foot on the pedal. Every time he reached for the pile of maps on her lap, she lifted her knee. Rivulets of heat raced up and down her spine.

He reached again. The expandable folder bobbed against the bottom of the steering wheel. Her breasts pebbled as a map passed her chest by inches. He dropped it in the folder. Her stomach dropped with it.

He didn't say a word. He didn't have to. He slid the entire folder off her lap. Evie inhaled sharply, her abdomen pulled board flat. He'd found Kentucky.

"Want me to read it?" he asked.

Her mouth tasted as if she'd been chewing paper. "I arranged this trip to see what a woman traveling alone might encounter. If I was on my own, I'd have to read it myself."

"At seventy miles per hour?"

She raised her toe off the gas pedal. "Sixty-five."

"You could use me."

Let me count the ways. She cleared her throat. "Sorry but you're strictly for emergencies."

"What am I, a set of jumper cables?"

He'd given her libido a jump start.

She grinned at his wry sense of humor. "My editor, my parents, and basically everyone I know insisted I have a mechanic come along. I told them it was a brand-new car."

"Those can be the worst."

"So they say. If it hadn't been for those rest-stop muggings last month, I'd be doing this alone."

"Mm."

"You sure you don't mind if I do most of the driving?"

"That's fine."

Once more, curiosity got the better of her. She studied him out of the corner of her eye. She'd rarely met a man who didn't take control the moment he entered a car. Most of them went straight to the driver's side.

Cole was unique; his ego secure. He hadn't once pressed his foot to the floor when she braked late or gripped the armrest when she took a corner.

"I'm sure you'd do it very well," she reassured him.

He turned subtly. "Do what?"

"Drive. I wasn't questioning your driving."

"I didn't think so. You've never seen me in action. Behind the wheel, that is."

She listened to his western drawl. The man had no idea how sexy his voice was. "It's just, the way I set this up, I was going to be doing it alone. Doing something alone is very different from doing it together."

"You don't say."

"I meant traveling."

"It's a long trip, and we'll be going all the way together. Is that it?"

"Yes. Well, um, yes. In a sense." She gritted her teeth, her hands damp on the wheel. "Did any of that make sense?"

"Completely."

He laughed. She sighed. She hoped and prayed

she'd gotten through that thicket of potential double entendres without him catching onto them.

"And don't forget the motels," he added.

She jabbed the gas pedal. They surged forward. "That's one thing we won't be doing together. Sharing a room, I mean."

"Nothing to be afraid of there."

She eased her shoulders down from around her ears. They rose gradually of their own accord as a nagging thought occurred to her. Had he meant she shouldn't worry about him taking advantage? Or did he mean he wasn't the least tempted?

Her consternation, and a lead foot, sent the speedometer to eighty. She eased up. She glanced over. Without moving his head, he watched the needle edge its way down. "Just seeing how she handles," Evie explained.

"She?"

"Don't all men refer to cars as she?"

"You're not going to name it, are you?"

Beneath that laconic delivery he had a very dry sense of humor. Jumper cables indeed. She grinned, relaxing by degrees. A friendly, teasing tone might be just what they needed. "Actually I was thinking of calling her Conchita."

"Conchita the Conquest?"

"Better than Norman the Conquest."

He groaned. She'd gotten him to smile! She should write this down. She compared the twinkle in his eyes to the stars outside. So what if he felt no need to offer editorial comment on every car and driver they passed?

The strong silent type might be a godsend on a long journey in confined quarters.

A mile passed. She wondered if he was quiet in bed too. "Whoa."

He sat forward. "Something wrong?"

Just the fact that the rippling of his flannel shirt made her picture a washboard of abdominal muscles beneath. Not to mention the enticing smell of him, his palpable physical presence, his voice, his— "Nothing's wrong," she chirped.

And nothing would happen. She'd thrown herself heart-first into too many relationships. Her consumer articles may have given her a first-class education in the ways people could be bilked, hornswoggled, or hood-winked, but when it came to men, Evie wore a sign saying LIE TO ME. She was too optimistic by half.

She hit the button for the radio. "How do we find a music station?"

"Press scan."

If only she could scan a list of available men that easily. She'd listen a few minutes then switch to the next. And the next.

No, you wouldn't, an inner voice scolded. *You'd listen to the first and believe every word he said.*

Cole leaned forward, jerking her attention back to the dim array of buttons on the control panel. "You turned up the heat."

And to think she'd blamed her zooming tempera-ture on him.

"Hit this. If you find something you like, press it twice and it'll stay there."

"And if I click my heels three times, will I end up back in Kansas?"

"Only if it's on the itinerary." He hardly smiled.

She grimaced and drove on. Ten miles from the Tennessee state line she gave small talk one more try. "Too bad about Bud."

"Yeah."

Long pause.

"If it weren't for his back going out on him, we wouldn't have gotten off to such a late start."

Cole grunted. "If it weren't for his back, we wouldn't be here period."

"I wonder how he'll manage the garage without you."

"Vivian's there."

"She knows as little about cars as I do."

"She's a pretty shrewd diagnostician."

"Really?"

"She's a good translator."

"I didn't know she spoke Spanish."

He chuckled, a rusty throaty sound. "She speaks Engine. If somebody comes in and says their car's making a funny noise, *rrr*, *rrr*, or *k-chunk*, *k-chunk*, she can tell right off what they mean. I keep telling Bud he should name her Customer Liaison. He says if he did, she'd want a raise equal to the title."

Evie laughed. "Bud would look at it that way."

"After twenty-five years married to a mechanic, Vivian probably knows more about cars than either one of us. People often know more than you give them credit for."

Evie nodded. *Diagnostician. Liaison.* They weren't

words she'd expected from Cole. Neither was that one little word *us*. Fiddlesticks. She wasn't looking for kicks on Route 66. Cole was her travel partner, nothing more. Nevertheless, she decided to reward him for opening up. "You can be very funny, you know that?"

"Yeah."

He was dead silent for the next hour.

You're funny, she'd said. As far as Cole was concerned, he was nuts.

Bud's so-called strained back had started that morning as a groin pull from a pickup basketball game. In a quick conversation with Vivian, it had magically evolved from a pull to a strain to full-blown back spasms. To hear her tell it, Bud was aging faster than a vampire in sunlight.

Cole hadn't believed a word. He wondered if it was a good thing knowing your friends were bad liars. He wasn't reassured. Bud and Vivian were warm, loving people who'd always done their best to run his life as they saw fit.

By the time Evie had driven up in her showroom-shiny Conquest, he knew it was too late to mutter his customary "not interested." The minute he saw her, there didn't seem any point in telling this beautiful, poised, smiling stranger he wasn't interested in meeting women.

Evelyn Mercer had to know he'd been ducking her for two years. Every time she and her dad stopped by the garage to kibitz with Bud about car repairs, Cole found a convenient excuse to straighten air filters in the storage room or stack retreads out back.

He'd been heading that way when Vivian had shooed him onto the asphalt out front. His hands had been black. Evie hadn't hesitated. She'd extended her hand, beamed a smile at him, and given him a nod. "Nice to meet you, Cole."

He'd mumbled something unmemorable. Words didn't matter. Her look did: layers of chestnut hair, dramatic dark slashes for eyebrows, a laughing glint in her blue eyes. She wore a two-piece suit with a short skirt. He'd noted that her legs didn't totter on high heels.

Cruising down I-75 ten hours later, he glanced at those nylon-clad legs. The dash's green glow highlighted a knee. Her ankles were in shadow. His mind was in the gutter.

He took it back to that morning. After the usual pleasantries, he'd gone inside to wash the grime off his hands. Then as now he'd told himself she'd planned this trip with fifty-year-old Bud. She wouldn't have needed that outfit to impress him; Bud worshiped her as if she were the daughter he'd never had.

Cole worshiped her as if she were the woman he'd never allowed himself to have.

Reality check: He was there to fix the car if it broke, check the tires, change the oil. What did it matter if after one look, one touch, he'd fallen head over heels, lightning-striking, once-in-a-lifetime in love with her? There wasn't a damn thing he could do about it.

TWO

They got to the motel after midnight. Evie insisted on checking in alone to rate the service for single women travelers. Cole waited outside. He'd spent an hour pinpointing the exact moment she'd stood his life on its head. What was another ten minutes?

He trailed inside as the clerk handed her her key. The man announced her room number and told her where to park around back.

Cole dawdled at the check-in. He paid for his room with the credit card the magazine had supplied, then went outside to haul his duffel bag out of the trunk. "Is there a problem?" he asked as she passed him in the parking lot.

"Letting a man overhear a woman's room number is poor security."

"I didn't think it was too swift sending you out here in the dark either."

"I'll make a note," she replied cheerfully. She seemed eager to get inside.

He stayed behind, dragging in lungfuls of fresh air, leaning against the trunk. No doubt someone would spot him lurking and call the cops. He loitered all the same, staring up at the window he pegged as hers. "What next, Creek, baying at the moon?"

He hitched his duffel onto his shoulder and trudged to the second floor. He stuck his key in the lock. An air conditioner hissed stale air. The artwork had been purchased in bulk. A blank television offered mute company. He'd heard a radio in Evie's room as he passed, a running shower. He pictured her naked, her body glistening with droplets of water.

He shook his head. A month in a car with Evie Mercer. At this rate he'd be chewing the upholstery before they got to Texas.

He threw his duffel on one of the beds. He reached for the telephone. He owed his good friend Bud a call for setting him up this way. The line was busy. He hung up, unpacked, tested the sag in the mattress. Hands behind his head, he stared at the acoustic ceiling. There'd been nights when he would have been glad of a roof over his head, much less a clean bathroom. He wondered if she was done with her shower.

He sat up fast. Okay, he'd check on her in ten minutes. In the meantime he gave himself whatever the opposite of a pep talk was. Evie was beautiful, confident, brave—that's how he'd seen her—willing to take on the world, to meet life head-on and shake hands with it.

Not like him. Skeptical, suspicious, and scarred weren't words he'd apply to her. From their first meeting she'd looked eager and energetic. "Face it, Creek, she'd looked."

He'd caught her casting sideways glances at him in the car, flitting looks, languid looks, looks that landed on his cheek like caresses, on his chest like a soft heated palm, on his thigh like a woman's thigh brushing his in a slow dance.

She was curious, interested, and spirited enough to give a man a shot. His stony silence had thrown her off her stride, which, judging from her driving, was usually full speed ahead. After that Gas-N-Go she'd been downright agitated.

He didn't want to upset her. He'd scrape his knuckles across engine blocks rather than hurt her. But it wasn't guilt eating at him like old rust. It was the flash of insecurity he'd seen on her face when she couldn't get through to him, the hint of vulnerability he would've never expected and couldn't resist.

The telephone rang. He grabbed the receiver. He needed a wake-up call, any excuse to get her off his mind. It was Evie. She needed help.

Before she hung up he was knocking at her door. She answered, huffing a strand of hair off her forehead, pulling her terrycloth robe shut.

She greeted him with a wail of frustration and a cockeyed smile at her own histrionics. "It's this TV. I can't get a thing. I tried cable, noncable, every button on the remote. . . ."

She smelled of soap. He smelled fire. He ambled inside. "What's the problem?"

"The picture. I never expected snow in Tennessee."

He thumped the set with his palm. "You staying up?"

She tightened the sash on her robe. "I was wound up after the drive. Aren't you?"

Worse than a travel alarm.

The TV balanced on a stand beside the dresser. Poking around behind it, Cole noticed her shoes at the foot of the king-size bed. The telephone sat propped on a pillow. He wondered who she'd been talking to. Probably the man at the front desk.

She hovered, her hair sweeping across her shoulder as she leaned over to see. "Well?"

"Give me a minute."

Moist heat floated out of the bathroom. He caught sight of something silky hanging from the shower rod. He crouched, punching two buttons on the back of the set. "There."

"That's it?"

"That's it."

"I thought I'd miss *Letterman* for sure."

He stretched his legs and sidled out from behind the set.

She swept her hair up with one hand, holding it back as she graced him with a thankful smile. Barefoot, close up, she was inches shorter. The robe gaped slightly, revealing a piece of lace trim curving over a softly molded breast. "I never knew having a personal mechanic would come in so handy." She laughed.

"What's the Groucho Marx line? 'I'd love to rotate your tires, but you'll have to stay in the garage overnight.' " He waggled his brows.

She laughed again. It was one big joke. Nothing untoward, nothing dangerous. He was being helpful, friendly, neighborly. So why wasn't he moving?

Her gaze darted to the carpet. His landed on her bare feet, those knocked-over shoes.

"Thank you again." She smiled.

"You're welcome."

Her dramatically dark brows rose. "See you in the morning?"

"Yep."

He glanced at the bed. He pictured waking up beside her, the light soft on her oval face, her skin bare beneath the rumpled sheets. He'd throw his arm around her shoulders, cuddling her warm body into the curve of his, inhaling the scent of her mussed chestnut hair.

Loneliness opened in him like a long dry well. It was the contact he longed for as much as the sex.

"Cole?"

He looked in her eyes. Who was he kidding? Was there half a chance in hell she was as lonely as he was?

It might explain all that talk in the car, the effort she'd put into reaching out.

"Cole?"

He blinked. "Sorry. Been staring at too many white lines."

She nodded at the bed. "At least the sheets aren't striped. Or lined with mile markers."

"Wonder how many miles people have put on that mattress?"

Her smile faltered.

He ran a hand across a jaw that rasped like sandpaper. "Forget I said that."

"No problem. Long day."

After that example of gutter thinking he saved her the trouble of showing him the exit by backing to the door. Her bare feet padded across the carpet behind his cowboy boots, innocent as whispers, suggestive as sighs.

She paused in the open door, one hand sliding down the jamb, the other curling around the brass knob. "Well, 'night."

" 'Night."

"You're down the hall?"

"Yep."

"You look tired."

"I'll be fine." He turned to go.

"Cole?"

He wasn't sure he wanted to see the look that went with that tone of voice. Inquisitive, inviting, reluctant to let him go. This was all his fault. If he'd talked to her in the car, neither of them would be in danger of confusing loneliness with longing.

He turned.

Her eyes were dewy, her head angled apologetically. "I'm sorry we got off to a rocky start."

Her lipstick was mostly gone. He wanted to taste those naked lips.

"I know you didn't plan to come on this trip," she said.

He'd come with her anywhere.

The pun made him wince. And no, he hadn't planned this; he carried no protection whatsoever.

Maybe he should pick some up tomorrow. Maybe he should have his head examined.

He took one step toward her. He wanted to tell her; something had hit him today, he didn't know what it was or whether it would last. Whatever it was, she didn't want to get involved in it.

Then she lifted her chin and looked him in the eye. The woman would take on anything, eyes open, chin up. The closer he got, the firmer she stood her ground. "I think we could be friends."

Yes.

"I want us to be."

You got it.

She laughed. "Cole, maybe it's my imagination, but if you don't say anything, all I can do is picture what you're thinking. That could lead to misunderstandings."

"You want to know what I think?" She couldn't misunderstand what he was about to do.

She planted both feet and crossed her arms. "Shoot."

He took her face in both his hands. Her breasts rose as she sucked in a breath. But the shock he expected, even hoped to see in her eyes, never developed. A touch of frostiness in their blue depths melted faster than morning dew. Her lips pursed. Maybe she was going to say his name. He didn't wait to find out.

Angling her head back, he caught a whiff of her shallow breath. He needed to scare some sense into one of them, show her how raw and ragged it could be between them if they didn't stop it.

His plan worked like a charm—right up until the

moment his lips touched hers. His rough intentions fell apart faster than petals off a wilting rose. Instead of a savage rake, his lips stayed tender. His palm never strayed to her breast. His hips never shifted. The shower's heat melded with her body heat. A sultry aroma of jasmine rose from her skin. Her tongue met his, tentative but not coy. He got the heart-sinking sensation she wanted this as much as he did. Hell.

A moan rumbled deep in his chest.

She responded with a mew of her own. Her arms uncrossed. She gripped his shirt, slinking into the protective circle of his embrace.

He dragged in a breath, his lips hovering for one more kiss. He glanced down, tempted. Her robe was crushably soft, her lingerie creamy and delicate against her skin. He pictured it sticking to her damp flesh, wet and transparent. He stepped back.

Her eyes fluttered open. "Cole?"

"You don't have to say it." His voice grated like a bad gearbox.

The surprise in her eyes withered. "I—I don't know what to say. I never expected this."

Try falling in love on a Monday morning in September. His head pounded. The way she blinked and laughed, he would have bet hers spun. Her cheeks flushed. Her eyes widened.

"I never expected—" She drew the tip of her tongue across her lips as if astonished to find a taste of him there. "Not that I'm complaining." She laughed. "It's just—"

It was just nuts. She wasn't backing down or pushing him out the door. She should have been. Some angels rushed in where men knew better than to tread. One fool in love was enough. He leaned a fist on the doorjamb and stared hard at the carpet. "You don't want this."

"I can decide that for myself."

"Decide this." He pulled her body blatantly close. He crooked one arm around her waist, his other hand gripping her thigh through the robe as if testing a handful of flesh. "You don't waste time."

Her eyes flashed. She wrenched out of his arms. "I didn't say I'd go that far."

"You didn't say no."

"I'm saying it now." Her shoulders squared.

The motion drew his eye to the front of her robe. He'd never thought terry cloth seductive. Which only went to show that the right woman could make anything hot. He fingered the inside edge of one lapel. The work-roughened backs of his fingers traced the neckline down and in. Beneath her skin he felt the rapid patter of her heart. "You feel good. Want to know how I feel?"

He didn't know if it was the macho display or the leer that got her back up. A zing of anger jolted through her. Flinty pride hardened her features. A woman's weapons, fielded just in time.

"I suggest you go." Her voice was steady, her gaze level. He waited to see if it would stay that way.

She knocked his hand away and folded one lapel over the other. Skimming a strand of hair off her flaming cheek, she buried her hand in the crook of her arm.

He decided to top off the tank, to make sure the stoplight stayed lit for the rest of their trip. He leaned arrogantly against the doorjamb, arms dangling, hands folded lazily over the evidence of his desire. "Our little car ride would be nothing compared to the ride I could give you tonight. I could take you a lot farther than Kentucky." He crooked a brow.

Her expression changed. With a sinking feeling he realized she'd seen through the cheap machismo for the act it was. She knew he'd done it to drive her off, to run away.

It wouldn't be the first time.

He mumbled a brusque good night, turned, and strode down the hall. He waited for the trigger-cocking click of a lock, the gunshot of a door slamming behind him. It never happened. Instead he felt her troubled gaze every step of the way.

In the motel restaurant the next morning Evie chose a booth with a view of the lobby. She wanted to see him coming before he spotted her. She needed every second she could scrounge to prepare herself.

Pawing at sugar packets, she tapped a plastic stirrer against her notepad. SERVICE AND THE SINGLE WOMAN, the heading read. Instead of notes on her waitress's attentiveness, she found herself rewriting possible opening lines:

So, you're finally up, she'd say.

Horrible. Open to any number of suggestive comebacks. She crossed it out instantly.

So, that was some act you put on last night.

Too accusatory. Besides, *she* hadn't been acting when she'd responded to his kiss. What was *her* excuse?

She stared at the rapidly filling page, then ripped it from the notebook. She tossed the wadded paper in an unused ashtray and immediately started writing again.

"I thought we'd head west today." Too upbeat. Too "let's pretend nothing happened."

What had happened? Could someone tell her that? Until she knew she couldn't share a pot of coffee with the man much less another eleven hours in a car.

Our little car ride would be nothing compared to the ride I'd give you.

Her blood chilled at the memory. Crudeness wasn't like him; her panicked telephone call to Bud had confirmed that. She hoped she hadn't worried her old family friend. She also hoped, prayed, and fervently wished this burgeoning fiasco wasn't somehow her fault. Why else would someone as calm, even-tempered, and honorable as Cole Creek reduce himself to playing the macho jerk? Was he desperate to get rid of her? Had she been throwing herself at him? Had she sent the wrong signals? Again?

She grimaced and dropped her pen. She was not going to hurl herself into another relationship. Yes, she'd been flattered when he'd kissed her. She'd been curious, hopeful even.

She twisted a sugar packet left and right. He was a wonderful kisser, tender, powerful, restrained. She imagined him as a lover. The packet ripped, spraying granules everywhere. She groaned.

"Be there in a minute," the waitress drawled, gliding by with a tray.

Evie's apology froze in her throat. Cole stood at the checkout counter. His hair was finger-combed and honey-colored. Drumming his fingers on the marble, he pursed his lips. She remembered his kiss all the way to her toes. He'd held her as if he hadn't held a woman in a thousand years.

She read his lips. "Checking out," he said to the clerk.

"I'd check him out, too, honey. Ooh-wee." The waitress stood over her, a coffeepot in each hand. "You want coffee with that cream?"

She'd nervously opened half a dozen thimblefuls of cream and dumped them all in her cup. "Sure."

The waitress poured. Evie was intensely grateful; she couldn't have managed the cup much less a pot. Her entire body seemed racked by fine tremors. It was as if someone had turned on an electric current. She knew who.

Cole sauntered their way. He walked like a cowboy, a hip-swaying swagger that drew her attention to his jeans. She averted her eyes. His heels hit the ground with fixed deliberateness. She watched those scuffed leather boots close in. He slid into the booth opposite her.

"And what'll you have—sugar?"

He took the waitress's flirty tone in stride. "I'll have whatever the lady's having."

The waitress slid over a saucer filled with cream servings.

Nobody laughed. The two of them stared at the tabletop, glancing now and then across the Formica abyss. The waitress slapped down a couple of laminated menus. "I'll be back when you're ready. To order, that is."

Evie's face flushed.

Cole watched her from behind an invisible barricade. Deep in those wary blue eyes he punished himself for uncommitted sins. She wanted to tell him it was all right. She'd given him the wrong impression, done everything wrong, kissed him back.

"You're up early," he said. His voice was husky, unused until now.

It'd be like that every morning.

Evie smiled. "I never sleep well in a strange bed." Especially when she was bedeviled by thoughts of the stranger who might have shared it.

She tore her gaze away. She was so lucky; she'd been so close to getting carried away.

His kiss had been so gentle, filled with such need.

Thanks to her impulsive, brazen reaction, that sweet kiss had become raw, personal, too revealing too fast.

Wasn't that usually *her* problem?

That's why he'd retreated behind the crude act. He'd been embarrassed. He recognized "too fast" even if she didn't.

She wasn't offended. On the contrary, she understood completely. She'd driven off more than one man by rushing into things.

There was this one tiny hitch that prevented her from explaining any of it. One deep dark secret she'd take to her grave. Yes, she'd been shocked at his kiss, his raw frankness. But shock fades. Deep in the night she'd had to admit his blunt sexuality had stirred something in her, something primal and purely physical. Every time she tried to sleep she'd seen the smoldering dare in his eyes, pictured the furious ride they'd have.

For the hundredth time she reminded herself his vulgar dare hadn't been a come-on. It had been a barely concealed "go away."

Take the hint, honey.

She fixed him with a determined smile. "I'm sorry I gave you the wrong impression last night."

He tossed one of her empty creamers in the ashtray. "You didn't give me anything I didn't ask for."

Her pale coffee curdled in her mouth. "The best explanation I can come up with is that the confined space of the Conquest, all that time crammed together, created a false air of intimacy."

"False airs," he repeated.

It had been one of her longer opening lines. She dug the hole deeper. "Prolonged closeness can sometimes create weird static electricity between people. Who knows? Maybe it was that stuff they spray in cars to make them smell new."

"Fumes and false airs."

"Right."

He sipped some more.

"You have a better theory?"

"How about lust?"

There it was again—gruffness pushing her away. The hunger in his eyes drew her right back.

The waitress set down a pile of toast. Cole leaned back. "Thanks." He picked up a slice. The knife's edge scraped as he glided a pad of butter across the coarse surface. He watched it melt.

Something melted inside Evie. Every scent, every

sensation seemed multiplied. She watched his finger-tips balance the toast. His other hand closed around the knife. Spreading butter to every edge, he didn't miss a spot. He licked a dripping dot off the crust. She watched his lips, a flash of white teeth. He tore off a corner. The crunch reverberated through her.

His gold lashes rose. For a heart-stopping moment he looked back.

Grabbing her own slice of toast, she crunched furiously. "I just hope I didn't mislead you. I never intended to."

He grimaced as if the coffee had suddenly turned bitter. "Did I say that?"

"I got the feeling you were trying to scare me away."

"I never said that."

"I want a mechanic. That's all."

A wry smile crossed his lips. "Like I said, I'd be happy to rotate your tires."

She flattened her lips into an unamused line. "This stops here, Cole."

He scowled out the window at the few remaining trucks in the parking lot. "All appearances to the contrary, you *can* trust me."

"According to Bud, you're the most honorable man he knows." Her tone implied she doubted it.

Cole seconded those doubts. "What would Bud know about it?"

"He's been your boss for two years. You live above his garage."

He poured a thimble of cream into what remained of his coffee. Nudging the container into the ashtray, he dislodged her wadded-up note. "What Bud says isn't always the most accurate."

"Are you saying he's a liar?"

"I'm saying he tends to describe me in very flattering terms. He does the same for you. According to him, you're smart, funny, ambitious, and working your way straight into the editor's spot at some socially involved magazine."

She modestly tucked a strand of hair behind her ear. "I don't know if I'd go that far."

"You're also well past marrying age, and in his humble opinion, you could use a good man. He says the ones you've found so far haven't been any kind of match for a woman of your caliber."

She laughed weakly, the heat rising to her cheeks. "You know Bud. He thinks everyone should settle down."

"He thinks the world of you."

"You too." An uncomfortable silence stretched.

"So," Cole said, "we're agreed Bud can exaggerate when it comes to people he likes."

"Sounds like it."

"Just don't believe everything he says about me." Cole tossed back his coffee then nodded to a tractor-trailer rig pulling out of the parking lot. "If you want me to hitch a ride back to Michigan, I can manage."

"No." Her hand shot out and rested on his arm. "I never said that. I need a reliable mechanic."

"Just not the rest of it."

"Right."

"In that case—" He shifted his gaze to his arm.

She withdrew her hand as if burned. Her cheeks flamed.

Cole folded his arms, planting his elbows on the table. He scooted forward on the seat. "Look, I've got a box of tools, a manual, and a spare in the trunk. Do you really think that'll do it if something goes wrong with your car? We'd probably be on some deserted stretch of I-80 in the dead of night and it'd be something I didn't have the parts for."

She pictured them stranded, two people, a lonely stretch of road. They'd huddle for warmth.

"What you need is a cellular phone and a tow truck."

What she needed was a hormone depressant. She was the problem; fantasizing, daydreaming. This was an assignment, not a blind date. "I'm sure we can manage the closeness in the car as long as we face up to it."

"Meaning?"

"A man and woman, far from home—the circumstances created a sense of curiosity, a desire to learn a little more about each other."

"Did you want more?" He asked it so carefully.

The words whispered in her mind. Did she? "No. It was an experiment, that's all. We shouldn't have."

"We didn't."

"See? We're adults. As long as we recognize the chemistry, and there is chemistry, that's normal, we're two healthy people. As long as we deal with it sensibly and frankly, then we won't have a problem." She laughed. "What's a little sexual awareness between adults?"

"What's a lot?"

The crackle she heard wasn't sparks shooting across the table, it was him playing with the crumpled piece of paper he'd picked up from the ashtray: her notepaper covered with opening lines for this conversation.

Caffeine slammed into her system. She snatched the paper, crushed it in her palm, and swept their litter into the ashtray. "We've got to get going."

Watching her flurry of activity, he smoothly leaned forward to pick up the check.

She snatched that too. "The magazine'll get it."

"Whatever you say."

She'd said a mouthful. She dropped her keys, her pens, her brush, and her compact onto the table. She found her wallet hidden beneath a map. "Want to hear how far we're going today?"

He crooked a brow.

She flattened the map on the table, firmly squelching any suggestive thoughts. "We're going west, young man. Across Tennessee to Nashville, then down to Memphis. I was planning a short trip to Graceland—" A swift glance for catty comments.

No objections.

"—then after lunch we'll take 55 north to St. Louis. We should be there by sunset." She stuffed the map back.

"I thought New Orleans came next."

"Tropical Storm Roberto made other plans. He's sweeping up from the Gulf, dropping torrential rains on Louisiana, Mississippi, and Georgia. I thought we'd bypass all that and hit the Big Easy on the way back. We can see the Arch if we make good time."

"Sounds fine. What about us?"

She popped out of the booth. "No reason why we can't change course just as easily. Flexibility is the key." At the register she handed over a twenty and waited for change. "How would you like to drive this morning?"

He recognized the consolation prize for what it was. "You'll read the map?"

"Got it right here."

"Deal." He held the door for her.

"Oh, and Cole?"

His fist tightened on the handle as she turned those imploring blue eyes his way. "Yeah?"

"Promise me you'll talk more."

He rasped out a breath. "I'll try."

Fiona found herself listening, intently, purposefully. It was as if the sound of the rain wanted to speak to her, as if its pattering code of dots and dashes held some urgent message.

But the message wasn't for her.

She turned the radio down and closed her eyes, opening herself to the elements, to life-giving water and dim soothing light, to the spaces between the raindrops. A message was waiting for—

Eve. The woman who hadn't stayed on the line long enough to talk to her Monday night. Fiona had told her she was journeying toward her destiny, a destiny that was closer than she realized. Look in Ohio, Fiona had said.

She realized with a shock that rocked her sizable frame that she'd been utterly and totally mistaken. Oh, this was rare. She flattened her hands to the sides of her voluminous Hawaiian muumuu and listened again. Eve's soul mate wasn't in Ohio! He was in . . . Tennessee. No. Missouri? *Each time Fiona settled on a place, the planet shifted and the globe spun. She shuddered and shook her head.*

But what was she to do? There was no way to reach the woman with a correction; Austin in the Evening was booked solid for the rest of the week.

She planted her feet before the bay window and looked up. Raindrops fell like tears. Sky leaks, her nephew called them. She listened to the thunder in the distance. How could she have been so wrong?

Lightning tinted the sky. Static, Fiona decided. That must have been it. Static on a cosmic scale.

THREE

At ease, in command, Cole drove through the thinning morning traffic an hour outside Knoxville.

From her spot on the passenger's side, Evie challenged him. "You said you'd talk."

"What do you want to talk about?"

"You pick the topic."

"You said you wanted to pretend it never happened."

She'd said nothing of the kind. "We can pretend we've put it behind us."

He smiled grimly. "That's just about it. Pretending." He fixed her with those cool blue eyes.

"Cole."

"So find another topic. It's your car."

At the moment it felt more like a trap. She squirmed in her seat as he eyed her again. Hooking her fingers in her shoulder strap, she pulled it away from the side of her neck. It tugged against her breast. She felt Cole's gaze drop. "For starters," she declared, "it isn't my car."

"The magazine's, then."

"*Consumers' Risk Report*. Ever read it?"

"Bud keeps a copy in the waiting room."

"We emphasize what to look out for in children's toys, flammable electric blankets, car safety. Product safety."

"Uh-huh."

"I don't know how Bud got the idea I want to be editor someday."

"Maybe it's the way you say *we* when you talk about the magazine."

His tone, and Bud's assumption, nettled her. So what if she cared about her job? "It's a subject I think is vital," she declared hotly. "We're a consumer society. Someone has to look out for buyers. Old people get fooled by fast-talking salesmen. Kids get seduced by advertising for toys, sugary cereal, fruit juice with two-percent 'real' fruit. We've grown up expecting to be lied to, cheated, and sold products that will be obsolete in a year."

She caught the flicker of a smile cross his lips. Maybe she did get carried away. If he only knew some of the letters she'd gotten since her column started. "For instance, women practically *expect* to be sold a bill of goods when they buy a car. I'm doing a series on it."

"The black notebook?"

"Sneer all you want. We sent Brad to buy a Neptune Series E. He's a staff writer at *Consumer's Risk*."

"And?"

"I went to the dealer a week later. Same car, same

options. The best deal they offered me was five hundred dollars more than the deal they gave him. He wrote a column about it too. We have a his-and-hers op-ed feature every month."

"Is he single, this Brad?"

"That's not the issue."

If she'd noticed the way his grip eased on the wheel, she might have thought otherwise.

"And it doesn't stop at the dealer," she continued. "Women are cheated at brake shops, muffler shops, by mechanics in general."

"I try to be fair."

"I didn't mean you. In fact I've considered writing about you. And Bud. Finding an honest mechanic is like finding treasure, I can tell you."

He grunted and glanced in his sideview mirror at the hot rod passing them on the left. "I wouldn't know about that."

"You don't know how rare you are."

He flashed her a look.

The morning safely behind them, she felt confident enough to dare him. "Maybe I will write about you."

"Please don't. I couldn't handle the fan mail."

"I can see it now. 'Tonight on *Hard Copy*, the Last Honest Mechanic.'"

"There are others. You just have to know where to find them."

"Kind of like good men."

"Rare, huh?"

"Nearly extinct."

He formed a quick fist around the wheel. "Maybe you're right."

"You mean a good woman is hard to find?"

He'd meant there were a lot of bastards out there. A woman had to be careful. He shrugged. "A good woman might not be so rare—if a man took the time to look."

"Don't tell me you're not even looking."

Squinting at the gray sky, he kept his eyes on the road. "Looks like rain."

"Sounds like you're ducking the question."

"Great, now I'm sharing a car with Mike Wallace."

"Please. Diane Sawyer."

He grinned.

Evie did the same. She liked making him smile. "You've ducked me before, you know. Every time I showed up at the garage, in fact."

He groaned. He'd been afraid they'd get around to that.

"Am I that intimidating?"

"Hardly."

"Then why avoid me?"

They hit on the answer at the same time, replying in unison. "Bud and Vivian."

Evie laughed.

Cole huffed. "They'd have us married and on our honeymoon before we knew what hit us. Married people."

Evie amended that. "Happily married people. Even worse. They want everyone to be the same. Still . . ."

The tires hummed against the road. The radio played a country-western song about a no-good man. Against all his better judgment, Cole bit. "Still what?"

"Marriage isn't all bad."

"Isn't it?"

White lines zipped by like prison bars. The mile markers flashed past like a switch striping a child's backside.

"Cole?"

"What?"

"For a moment you seemed a million miles away."

"Only a couple thousand."

She considered the frown between his brows and attributed it to concentration. "You've avoided it so far. Marriage, I mean."

"So have you."

"You're not one of those men who sees the marriage knot as a noose, are you?"

"Could be."

"Running away from responsibility?"

He took his foot off the pedal so fast, they lurched forward. "Nobody's running," he stated flatly.

"I didn't mean it in a bad way."

"Is there a good way to run?"

She wondered. In the ensuing silence she studied his stony profile. An artery beat in his jaw. His attention stayed on the road, veering to the rearview mirror every now and then.

Unable to jump-start the stalled conversation, Evie calculated what time they'd reach Memphis. Refolding the map, she settled back in her seat. She crossed her legs and yanked on the back of her sweater where it bunched behind her. "The seats aren't bad."

"Pretty comfortable."

She scowled at the first drops of rain. Opening the

glove compartment, she pulled out a manual and flipped to the index.

Cole went directly to the knobs, twisting the first on his left. "There."

The wipers squeaked. Back and forth, back and forth. If she had to endure a hundred miles of that, she'd scream. "Mind if I turn the radio up?" She pressed scan. One talk show succeeded another down the dial. "Remember last night's topic? Men Who Can't Commit."

"The minute they started talking to that psychic, I tuned it out. Talk about bilking the gullible. You should do an article on that."

"I was thinking of it," she muttered glumly. Good thing they didn't rerun those shows.

Thirty miles passed. She untied her short boots and dug her toes into the carpeted mat. Every time she turned the heat up, Cole turned it down. Even woolly socks couldn't keep her toes warm. She tucked one foot under her thigh. Except for the suit she'd had no time to change the day before, she'd packed travel clothes, nothing binding or tight. These comfy old jeans fit like a second skin.

Cole glanced at the tear by her knee. The denim felt suddenly scratchy and overheated. She tugged on the patch by her pocket.

"Maybe the psychic was a bit much," she allowed. "But it might not be such a bad idea."

"Not committing?"

"Using the topics on talk shows as a jumping-off point for conversation."

Balancing his elbow on the windowsill, he drew a finger across his upper lip. "Do we have to?"

"Yes!" Evie scooted around in her seat to face him. "Today's topic: Do You Think It's True That Men Can't Commit?"

"You don't back down, do you?"

She had the night before, just in time to save herself a great deal of embarrassment. She unfastened her lap belt and turned completely toward him. Tucking both feet under her thighs, she sat back on her heels and hooked an arm around the headrest. "Well?"

He scowled at the automatic shoulder strap hugging her arm. "You could decapitate yourself with that."

"I trust your driving."

"What if we blow a tire?"

"They're brand-new."

"We could hit a rock."

"You could be as talkative as one. I need you here. Either we discuss commitment or we go back to marriage."

"Aren't they the same?"

"Do you think men are afraid of commitment?"

"I should have been committed before I ever agreed to this trip."

"Cole."

"Men can commit."

"A lot of women who called in last night didn't think so."

"Right, and they believed a psychic would help them."

"Maybe they were desperate."

"I'll say."

"Care to elaborate on that statement?"

It was like telling the executioner where to aim the ax. "I think a lot of men put the brakes on because they realize they've hooked up with the wrong woman. Hell, they may come right out and say so." He looked at Evie.

She raised her chin.

"And yet, when a man says he doesn't think a relationship's working, a woman will blame it on his inability to commit. Maybe the real point is that he doesn't want to commit to *her*."

Evie wriggled to get comfortable, edging her pert rear end toward the door handle. "You may have a point."

"The topic should be Women Who Refuse to Face Reality."

"Ah. So this is the woman's fault."

He winced. He knew full well this wasn't the kind of argument that anyone ever won. Nevertheless, he'd sworn high and low to himself the previous night that she'd be better off if she knew his faults first. He laid them out like a road map. "It takes two to ruin a relationship."

"I agree. To a point."

"What if he's not what she needs? Instead of telling him to take a hike, too many women dig in, they try to change the guy."

"Everyone can use improvement."

"When a man's wrong for a woman, why doesn't she just say so?"

"She may not want to hurt his feelings."

"Better than hanging on to something that'll never work. Anyway, a man knows. He knows he's being graded."

"That's not true."

"You could print a list like your magazine does. Check off all the qualities you like about a guy. This one's sluggish but dependable. This one's way too fast."

"Too hard to handle?"

"This one's got a good body, but—"

She grinned. "But he's carrying a spare tire—right around his middle."

They laughed together.

He draped his arm over the wheel, his wrist dangling. "You could put out a special issue of your magazine. 'The Male Risk Report.'"

"No woman should buy a man unless he comes with a manual." She popped open the glove box and pretended to read aloud from hers. "Caring For Your New Man. Oil and lube jobs. Engine maintenance." A twinge of curiosity rippled through her. "I wonder how many miles he's got on him?"

"Too many."

Sighing, she tossed the manual back. "It'd never work. Every man's different. It would be impossible to rate them in any systematic study."

"Some women do. They're not above a test-drive either."

"And you're saying men are?"

He shot her a look.

She'd been joking. He didn't take it that way. She

sat back down, unkinking her legs. So there had been a couple of men who'd used her. It took two to tango, as the saying went. She'd been happy, even eager, to make the relationships work. "When it comes to ratings, maybe women aren't picky enough."

Cole thought a minute. "I've had a few dissatisfied customers."

Her brows shot up. "Women? Not satisfied with you?"

"Thanks for sounding surprised."

She meant it. "What could anyone criticize about you?"

He slanted her a look. "They wanted me to talk more."

After a stunned pause she burst into laughter that rippled for miles. "Touché, Creek."

He grinned, clamping his hand over the fingers she'd rested on his arm. Seconds passed. A happy silence settled over them.

"Am I being a pain?"

He considered the warm tingle starting up beneath his flannel sleeve. "No."

"I don't want to bug you. We've got a long trip ahead of us."

"And we'll be going all the way."

She wagged a finger at him. "That's a double entendre. Remember what I said about sexual awareness?"

"We should go along with it."

She tilted her head, pondering whether that was how she'd put it.

"So how far would you go?" A smile played around the edges of his eyes.

"How far would I go with you?" She leaned toward him provocatively, enunciating precisely. "Thousands and thousands of miles. From coast to coast and border to border."

"And you expect me to keep this up all the way? My end of the conversation, I mean."

She playfully punched him on the arm. "Since you put it that way, you are officially requested to keep it up all the way."

He shook his head sadly. "I'd hate to disappoint you."

"I take it talk is not your strong suit."

"I'm a bit of a loner."

"Born that way?"

"Made."

Evie pondered his admission. Another cryptic clue. She decided not to follow it up. Better to preserve their informal mood. "Tell me more about yourself. That's an easy topic."

"I don't know."

"You don't know yourself?"

"Don't know where to start."

"You were born——?"

"In Montana."

"Lived there long?"

"Till I was sixteen."

"Where did your family move after that?"

He raked the road with his eyes. "Graceland. That's where we're headed, right?"

Evie wasn't sure where they were headed. Every time they got a conversation started, it came to a road-block. "It'll be at least an hour. Just stay on this road."

"Got it."

She reached in the back for her box of tapes and popped in the *Graceland* tape by Paul Simon. "This should last till we get there."

"Great."

Not another word was spoken until they pulled off the exit ramp an hour later and merged with the tour buses. Near the white-and-green gates of Graceland a mob of tourists waited in the rain.

"A Tuesday at noon and look at the crowds," she said to Cole. "It's like a shrine."

"Hope you brought an umbrella."

They huddled beneath it on the sidewalk. The nearness did nothing to span the gulf that had opened so mysteriously between them. Evie wondered where they'd gone wrong. They'd been talking about his family.

"America the weird," Cole said as they peered into the Jungle Room half an hour later. "What do you think the appeal is?"

"He did some great songs."

"I agree, but this—these women worship him."

They people-watched, noting the blissful stares, the devotion, the occasional tears. Evie looked at Cole, dry-eyed and leery.

One woman in particular had caught his eye. A middle-aged brunette, her chic bun streaked with gray, she had the thin hatchetlike face common to the Appalachians. She looked like a pioneer woman, someone who'd suffered but still believed. Her thin bowed shoulders straightened with every step she took through the King's domain.

"You're staring," Evie warned under her breath.

He knew it. He looked away in disgust. On the steps outside, he picked up the silent conversation he'd been having with himself. "That's the problem with love. Blind, unconditional, unreturned, and unreturnable. Doesn't she see he'll never love her back? Some women don't know when they deserve better."

"Cole?"

He pierced her with a stark look. "Women who love too much. Isn't that a topic on one of your talk shows? It's the truth. It's also the main reason I'll never get married."

They picked up Highway 55 and headed north, cutting across a corner of Arkansas. In a little over an hour they were in Missouri. They'd gotten fast food for lunch. Evie ate half of hers then stuffed it in the bag.

A passenger once more, she itched to pry beneath the surface. Why had he gotten so defensive? A lot of men didn't like the idea of marriage. It had been a topic, not a proposal.

She stared out the windows at the rain. The wipers slapped in time to another Paul Simon song. "Homeless" was its title. Cole reached over and turned it up.

He stared at the bleak drizzle and thought of the times he'd been homeless. He'd think of anything to banish that woman's face from his mind, that look of adoration—and loss. She knew her love was one-sided. So why didn't she stop? Why didn't she go somewhere else, meet someone who could return her feelings?

"Why don't you leave him?" the boy begged, trying to get her to stop crying, trying to coax her out the door before his father came home.

"You don't understand," his mother said. "I love him. He's your father."

He scowled and scraped a palm across the back of his neck. Most of the people in that place were just fans, normal, well-adjusted people. And most marriages weren't the hell his parents' had been.

Cole had hated his father as far back as he could remember. Mostly for the way he'd treated Cole's mother. He would hit her, belittle her, ignore her. Despite everything, she never stopped loving him.

He shook his head, breath hissing out from between his clenched teeth. He'd never understand it. Women didn't need love. What they needed were limits, rules, boundaries. They needed to demand more of the men in their lives and love them less.

He glanced over at Evie. She dozed in her seat, her head tilted back against the headrest, her lips parted. No danger of her loving him. The happy sparkle in her eye had died out after Graceland. He told himself to be glad it was gone.

That's when he saw the kid. A teenager, thumb out, backpack sagging off his shoulder, a plastic parka disguised everything else about him. He stood on the muddy shoulder, soaked by the drenching rain.

Cole cursed. He didn't want to stop. The last thing

he wanted was to look at this bedraggled kid up close. He especially didn't want Evie seeing him.

"Why not?" he asked, sneering. He'd told himself a million times a woman ought to see the bad side of a man before she got too involved. Evie needed to see his.

She sat up, squinting through the downpour. "Why are we stopping?"

Cole threw his right elbow over the seat and backed down the shoulder. Gravel crunched beneath the tires. He stopped beneath an overpass. Sheltered from the rain, a sudden silence enveloped the car. He peered through the spattered rear window. A hooded figure jogged their way.

"Oh no," Evie said.

"He needs a ride."

"I don't pick up hitchhikers."

"There're no prison signs in the area. None that I noticed," he muttered.

"That's not the point. No single woman in her right mind would pick up a hitchhiker."

"You're not single and you're not alone."

"But if I was—"

"He needs a ride."

"Cole. I don't mean to pull rank, but I'm leading this expedition and I am not picking him up."

"Fine."

She sat back.

"I am." He jabbed a button on the driver's armrest and unlocked the back door. A whoosh of highway sound, rain, and wind entered the car, along with a soaking-wet figure. The car rocked. Evie lowered her visor, eyeing their passenger in the mirror.

The boy whipped the hood off his head. His long hair was slicked back, matted by grease and rain. A scruffy beard, barely grown in, contrasted with his innocent pink cheeks. He looked fifteen at the most. "Hey, man."

"Hey," Cole said.

"Where you headed?"

"Where you going?"

The boy glanced from a tight-lipped Evie to Cole. "Anywhere."

Cole turned and put the car in first. "Anywhere's fine with me. How's St. Louis?"

"Great."

"Hold on just a minute." Evie touched Cole's arm, then twisted around in her seat. "Do your parents know where you are?" she demanded.

The boy rolled his eyes.

"I'm serious."

"They won't miss me," he said in quiet disgust.

"How can you say that?"

A touch of shame colored his cheeks. "Because I know."

"How old are you?"

"Old enough."

"All right?" Cole said, putting an end to her interrogation.

"No, it is not all right."

He pulled out onto the highway.

Evie muttered dire imprecations under her breath

for the next ten miles. "Of all the bullheaded, stubborn, naive—" At the first exit sign, she spoke up. "Stop here."

Cole didn't reply. The exit neared.

She drew a breath, ready to demand he pull over.

He flipped on his turn signal. "We need gas," he announced to no one in particular.

They rolled down the exit ramp into a station with an attached convenience store. Evie had her door open before they came to a complete stop. A warning buzzer went off. She raised her voice above it. "I'd like to talk to you, Cole."

He yanked on a lever under the steering column. The hood popped. He shoved open his door and came around the front.

Arms crossed, toe tapping, Evie waited. "I don't want him in the car."

"Too late."

"I don't trust him."

"Why? Because he's dirty? Because he's young?"

"Because he's lying."

Cole found the latch and lifted the hood overhead, blocking their argument from view. "Okay, what did he say?"

She threw her hands in the air. "You heard him. He said his parents don't miss him. If that isn't an out-and-out falsehood—"

His face grew hard. "Maybe it's true." The emptiness in his eyes was like a hole cut into darkness.

Evie froze. The misgivings she'd had since Graceland came back in full force; she didn't understand him. In plain fact, she didn't know him any better than she knew this hitchhiker. For better or worse they were sharing this car. She'd almost shared a lot more with him in her motel room.

She stood her ground. "I do not want to do this."

"Tell you what. You drive, and I'll sit shotgun and watch his every move. Will that make you happy?"

His sneering tone made her blood boil.

"There is nothing wrong with a little caution. He could be on drugs."

"He isn't." He stepped around her to whip a blue paper towel from a dispenser. Leaning over the fender, he twisted off the oil cap. "I'll check the oil."

"You are not changing the subject."

"We've got a car. He's got nothing but that backpack. What do you want him to do, sleep in a ditch?"

"There are agencies. Shelters."

He scoffed. "See any around?"

All she saw were fields.

Dragging the towel down the dipstick, Cole stabbed the bent metal into the hole marked OIL. He leaned his outstretched arms on the fender, his elbows locked. "Evie, think about it a minute—from *his* point of view. For one day he's going to catch a ride with a couple who isn't going to rob him, rip him off, or prey on *him*. He's safe."

The image mollified her for a minute. Then the car door opened and the slouching teenager headed for the convenience store. "Back in a minute," the kid mumbled sarcastically. "Don't wait up."

Evie bit her lip. She waited until he was out of

earshot. "But are we safe with him? He could be a thief, a mugger."

"I don't think so."

"You don't know anything about him."

Cole wiped the grime from his hands. "Evie, he's me."

FOUR

"He's what?"

Cole's voice grated. "He's me. I left Montana at sixteen and thumbed my way across the country. There were days I would've considered myself damn lucky to ride in a car like this."

He gripped the top of the dipstick as if to yank it out, then slowly withdrew it instead. He held it over the paper towel to show her. "Half a quart since yesterday. New cars can do that. You should keep an eye on it just in case."

She looked at him a long moment, then at the gas station. The kid roved up and down the aisles of the convenience store. "You keep an eye on it. I'm going to keep an eye on him."

Cole sighed and shoved the dipstick back. She treated the kid like a criminal. She "subtly" followed him down the aisles, standing behind him at the cash register. Cole recognized the sloping shoulders, the hanging head as shame and resentment built in their passenger. What did her tailgating accomplish? If the kid did pull a gun and rob the place, what could she do, write about it?

Cole squinted at the glistening engine. He remembered being so hungry, his insides ached. He'd envied anyone with the guts to take what they wanted and run. But he'd been too damn honest, too determined to live a life completely the opposite of his father's.

He shut the hood. Striding toward the rest room, he saw Evie pay for a submarine sandwich. It struck him as odd; she'd barely eaten what they'd bought in Memphis.

She slid it cross the counter to the kid. The band of tension around Cole's chest eased. For all her paranoia, she wasn't bad, just unfamiliar with the life.

When he came out of the bathroom the car idled beside the building. "Ready?" Evie called.

She'd taken the driver's seat as he'd suggested. He rode shotgun.

"So," he said to the kid as they pulled onto the highway. "St. Louis is where you're headed?"

The kid shrugged. Wedged into the far corner of the backseat by Evie's map case and his own troubles, he glared at the road whipping by. "It's okay."

"See you got a sub."

He folded the wax paper and stuffed half the sandwich in his pocket. "Yeah, thanks," he mumbled.

"You're welcome," Evie said slyly. She glanced up.

Cole reached over and flipped up her visor. The day was too gray to require a sunshade.

She shot him a look. She'd been using that to keep an eye on their passenger.

Everybody in the car knew it. Cole angled his shoulders toward the backseat. "So what's your name?"

The kid thought. "Brad. No, Luke. Luke."

"Okay, Luke. This road doesn't look too exciting."

"Are any of 'em?"

He crooked a weary smile. "How about if you catch some shut-eye? We'll wake you when we reach the city."

"Whatever."

For all his grumbling, the kid wrapped his coat around him and curled up. In minutes he was asleep. Cole turned on an easy-listening station.

Evie lowered her visor and took a peek. "Can we talk about this now?" she murmured.

"I couldn't leave him beside the road on a day like this."

"I meant let's talk about what you said."

He winced and stared straight ahead.

"I realize you're not any keener on personal revelation than Luke. If that's his name."

"Probably not."

"And you said he was honest."

"If he gives us his real name, he might get tracked down and sent home."

"Did that happen to you?"

A pause. "The first time. My dad beat me so bad, I couldn't walk for a week."

Evie said nothing, trying to absorb the shock. "I didn't know."

Cole accepted that, silently thanking her for the lack of pity.

"Will you tell me about it?" she asked quietly. She left it up to him.

He watched the hills go by. This section of the country looked familiar. But then, every highway looked the same. "I didn't have a family like yours."

"I haven't told you anything about my family."

"They produced you. They can't be too messed up."

She surprised him with a chuckle. "I think there's a compliment in there somewhere."

"I bet your parents have been together forever."

"High-school sweethearts."

"Waited until their wedding night to have sex?"

"That I wouldn't know."

"I bet they support you, talk to you every week, slip you extra money when you need it."

"I haven't needed a loan since my transmission died the month after I got out of college. I paid them back, though. With interest."

"I'm sure they knew you would. You're an only daughter, right?"

"I am not a princess. At least, I hope I'm not."

"You are."

She bristled.

"Just a bit," he said. "You've got that sense of entitlement, as if the world's going to measure up to your expectations."

"But my job is pointing out all the ways it falls short."

"Yeah. You see nothing strange about telling the whole world to shape up, make better stuff, live up to promises."

She shook her head, hair shushing across her shoulders. Proud but flustered, she added some perspective. "My family is far from perfect, Cole. Dad spends way too much money on his boat, and Mom's downright obsessive about housecleaning. And college! She's taking courses now. She has an egg timer she sets on her desk. Woe to anyone who interrupts her homework hour." Evie rolled her eyes. "They're not exactly the Cleavers."

They drove another few miles. She slanted a hesitant look his way. "We've gotten off the subject of your family."

He exhaled long and slow.

"Were they that bad?"

"I guess we weren't your typical white trash."

"Cole," she scolded.

He shrugged, glancing over his shoulder to satisfy himself that the kid was still asleep. "We were fairly well-off. My father was a cattle rancher."

"Was? Is he dead?"

"Yeah. Years ago. As for my mother, her full-time job was mollifying him. She died in ninety-one."

"I'm sorry."

"I wasn't. I was glad she outlived him. I always thought he'd kill her."

Maybe he was right. She found it difficult to imagine that kind of brutality. "Why didn't she leave him?"

"Because of her father, I think. They were dirt-poor. Dirt floor in their cabin, outdoor plumbing. She rode a broken-down pony to school. When she married my father and his four thousand acres, she thought he was the greatest thing that ever happened to her. The beatings were just the price she paid."

"I don't understand that kind of thinking."

"It might not even be true. Maybe she just loved him."

"How could she?"

"The way any woman does, unconditionally, in sickness and health. Even after he died she preferred memories of him to me."

"You can't mean that."

He dragged in a breath, the better to narrate a long story. "I ran away when I was thirteen. I'd been doing it for years in a way, going off to the mountains, camping out, anything to get away from the fights at home. She took a lot of beatings in my place. *She* protected *me*."

"Protecting their children is what mothers do."

"At thirteen her 'child' was nearly six feet tall. And a hundred and ten pounds. I ran off. I left her to him."

If he expected condemnation, he wasn't getting it from her. "Wasn't there anyone to turn to?"

"We lived on a ranch. Pretty isolated. The workers wouldn't tell on Dad—they'd lose their jobs. No one else knew except maybe my mother's sister. That's where I headed the first time, Aunt Aggie's house in Nebraska. They picked me up along the I-80. Like I said, I didn't walk for a week. He beat up Mom for crying about it. We laughed about it later, the two of us hobbling around the house like war victims."

He glared out the window, the better to avoid Evie's horrified look. "She told me I had to get away. One of these days it'd be him or me. All the while she insisted it wouldn't always be that bad. That was her motto. 'It'll get better.' She kept promising me.

"Then I met a girl in high school. I saw how a real family lived. One night, after a dance, Dad waited up for me. Instead of laying into me, he started picking a fight with Mom, slapping her around, punching her. I couldn't take it anymore. I hit him so hard, he went down cold." He swallowed. "I can still see her, on the ground, her arms around him, shouting at me to get out."

"I'm sure she didn't mean it. Women in that situation—"

"Women in that situation protect their abusers. Don't ask me why. They lie for them, lie to themselves. 'It'll get better. He'll change. Love will change him.' Love changes nothing."

"So you ran away."

"I was sixteen this time. I varied my route. I headed south to Utah, down through New Mexico and Texas. With all the illegal aliens, it's easy to find temporary jobs. Not so easy to make 'em pay you when you're done. I got to Nebraska after six months. There was a letter waiting from my mom. 'Don't come home,' it said. 'Whatever you do, don't ever come back.' "

Evie caught her lip between her teeth. She knew pity would be scorned. She turned toward the sideview mirror until her stinging tears evaporated.

Cole watched the road. "That's the story. That's how it ended."

Evie wondered if those stories ever ended. The past could be like a hitchhiker's worn duffel bag; Cole still carried his with him.

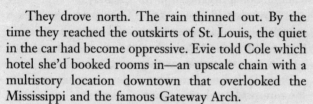

They drove north. The rain thinned out. By the time they reached the outskirts of St. Louis, the quiet in the car had become oppressive. Evie told Cole which hotel she'd booked rooms in—an upscale chain with a multistory location downtown that overlooked the Mississippi and the famous Gateway Arch.

Cole opened the map to the inset of St. Louis and figured a route through the business section.

"Before we stop," Evie whispered, "I want you to do me a favor."

He'd known something was brewing by the glances she'd bounced off her visor at their passenger. "What is it?"

"I accept your idea that sending Luke home isn't necessarily in his best interests."

He shot a look over his shoulder at the sleeping kid. The snoring had stopped a few miles back. The boy remained still.

Evie continued. "All the same, you'd know better than anyone the abuse these kids can run into on the street. What happens if the next person who picks him up isn't as nice as we are?"

He agreed. Honest, middle-class types rarely picked up hitchhikers. It was the weirdos one had to look out for, the ones on the prowl for skinny homeless kids who couldn't defend themselves. In a sick way he hoped Luke carried something, a knife, some pepper spray, anything to fight off the bad guys. "What do you suggest?"

"I suggest we stop at a gas station, look up the address of a shelter, and drop him off there. Isn't there some national organization for runaways?"

"Covenant House is one. They probably have a branch here." He wasn't sure it'd work. Like stray dogs, stray kids learned fast not to trust handouts. "There's a gas station coming up."

Evie pulled in. Leaving the gas pumping to Cole, she ran inside to leaf through a telephone book. Cole scraped a squeegee across the windshield. The pump dinged when the tank was full. He headed inside to pay.

Jotting down an address, Evie smiled at him as the bell on the door jangled. Her expression froze when she looked past him. "Where's he going?"

The kid had slipped out of the car. Slinking down the street, he cast a rapid glance over his shoulder.

"He's got my purse!" she yelled.

Cole shoved the door open and took off at a run. Evie was hot on his heels.

"Luke! Brad! Dammit, get back here!" His harsh voice echoed off the buildings. The few pedestrians cleared out of the way.

Within a block Cole had closed the distance. His feet pounding the ground, he reached out and grabbed the kid's collar. They went down in a grunting, tangled heap. Somewhere in the scuffle Luke caught Cole's kneecap with a solid kick. Cole hissed a curse beneath his breath, more at the fact that the kid had wriggled out of his grasp than at the pain.

Scrambling to his feet, Cole saw the kid zigzag to his right. Too late he saw why. A duffel the size of a punching bag hurtled his way. Unfortunately for the kid, running and throwing weren't his strong suits—he tripped and fell as he released the weight.

Unfortunately for Cole, his old football dodges were just as rusty. The duffel bounced on the sidewalk and caught him on the shin. Amazing how deeply padded deadweight could hurt. Cole swallowed the pain and limped around the bag. He cursed himself this time.

Of all the idiotic— He should have known better than to trust the kid. Hadn't he just told himself he'd once wished *he* had the guts to take what he needed?

The kid raced for an alley. Cole sped up. His boots weren't made for running. His shin ached; his lungs wheezed. He no longer heard Evie's running shoes slapping the ground behind him. Her outraged shouts had ceased two blocks earlier. He hoped she'd gone back to the station to call the cops.

Of course, an hour earlier he'd also hoped the kid had a weapon. Funny how wishes boomeranged.

The alley cut through to the other street. Evie had figured it out. While Cole and Luke had grappled on the sidewalk, she'd headed them off.

Barricaded behind a garbage can, Luke crouched as Evie closed in. He was cornered, not caught. The stubby penknife would see to that.

"Get back," Luke commanded. His voice cracked.

Unintimidated, Evie took a step forward.

"Get back!" Cole shouted.

The kid whirled. "Both of you. Stay back! I'm not going to any shelter."

"We're not going to hurt you," Evie said.

The soothing tone won her nothing but contempt.

"We want to help you," she insisted.

The kid told her what she could do with her help.

Cole's fists clenched. He was close to throwing the brat up against that brick wall and making him apologize—in detail.

The anger dissolved as rapidly as it appeared: He wasn't his father. His boots scraped across broken glass. Circling to his left, he gave the kid plenty of running room. "Take the money, leave the credit cards, and get out."

"No."

"Look," Cole said, "you can't sign a credit-card receipt as Evie Mercer, and you'd look damn stupid carrying a purse. The cash is all you need."

His gaze darting rapidly from one to the other, the kid tore open the purse, fished out Evie's wallet, and helped himself to the money. He bent the wallet double searching for hidden compartments. Photos and ID littered the ground. He tossed the eviscerated wallet on top of them.

Evie covered her mouth with her hand. She looked green. Cole was about to say something to her when the kid took off. Stepping back, Cole let him go. He grabbed Evie when she tried to follow. "Don't."

"He's getting away!"

Gripping her shoulders tight, he shook her. "It's only money."

"He stole my purse!"

"Whaddya want me to do? You want the gas-station guy to shoot him? You want him in jail with a bunch of perverts?"

Panting, furious, she gaped at him. "He's a criminal! Who cares what happens to him? What are you, some kind of Democrat?"

Her words hung over the alley.

"Actually," Cole rasped out, "I vote independent. When I vote."

The ridiculousness of it struck them both. Adrenaline translated into helpless laughter. When that faded, nerves took its place. Evie felt sick. She began to shake, her laughter fading into a hiccuping terror. "I can't believe that just happened. We got mugged."

"I got stupid. I should've watched him closer."

She scrabbled around in the garbage and litter, trying to put her purse back in order. Swiping at the tears blurring her vision, she hid her face when Cole crouched to help.

"I'm sorry, Evie."

"It's not your fault. You were nice to him. Nicer than I was. Maybe that's why he ripped us off—"

He gripped her arm. "This is *not* your fault."

She looked down at that angry fist. He released her instantly.

"I'm sorry," he said. He had the feeling he'd be saying it for a long time.

Evie stared at the Mississippi. She knew she'd sounded imperious and cold when she'd called his room. She'd summoned him to a meeting on the riverbank. The sunset wasn't the point. Neither was the water, muddy, wide, and slow flowing. They had to talk.

She stood on a flight of granite stairs leading down

to the water's edge. An array of flags lined the walkway. A man stepped up behind her.

She jumped.

"Still nervous?" Cole asked.

"Did you know the flood of ninety-two nearly drowned those flagpoles? Look how high they are."

"Uh-huh."

"Try to sound more excited. Things like that don't happen every day."

"Neither do muggings."

She rubbed her arms and shivered. She turned her back on him to look out at the water. "He had a knife."

"I know."

Cole would take every bit of the blame if she let him.

He took off his leather jacket, swinging it around her shoulders. She wished he wouldn't do that. It smelled strong and male and safe—like everything he was. She wanted to wrap herself in it. She dragged in the musky fortifying scent of him. "Cole?"

"Yeah?"

She laughed, although she felt like sobbing. "It seems pretty lame, doesn't it? All that talk this morning about lust and chemistry. If we'd been paying more attention to the road—"

"You think that was the reason?"

She whirled to face him. "You could have been killed."

"So could you. Dammit, Evie, he could've had a gun."

"Did you think of that when you tackled him on the sidewalk?"

He huffed and turned toward the water. Why couldn't she see the plain truth? "It was my fault. If anybody should know about protecting people from runaways, it's me."

"Like you should have protected your mother from your father?"

Tracing the Arch as it rose across the river, he peered into the distance. "I've read all the psychology, Evie."

"Bud says you read books on everything."

"More compliments from Bud?"

"From me too. You were very generous to pick up that kid and very courageous to race after him. You have no reason to feel guilty. About anything."

What about loving her? She'd been just about to tell him it wasn't going to happen between them when they got onto this subject. He remembered her words about lust and attraction—how pointless it seemed now. She was through with him before they'd even started. He'd wanted her to know what she was getting into. Fine. She was opting out.

"Maybe we should head inside," he said.

"Not yet." She clutched his coat around her. The neckline was nubby white wool, aged yellow over the years, mashed down by wear. She rubbed her cheek against it as if it were silk. Her lids fluttered shut.

Cole swallowed a knot of longing. "I'm sorry."

"I'm not." She stepped up to him. "Hold me?"

He put an arm around her. She fit herself to him, her cheek in the hollow by his shoulder. She felt warm and smelled even better. He closed his eyes and listened to the flags snapping in the breeze. Ropes dinged against poles like the rigging on old ships. He balanced his chin on her head then snuck a kiss.

She glanced up shyly. He couldn't help it. One kiss. To make up for everything else. To savor when the trip was over.

Her mouth molded to his, every sound drowned out by the pounding of his heart. When he let her go she licked her lips in lazy satisfaction. "Do you hear music?"

To his amazement, he did. A steamboat trolled by. Dixieland jazz floated across the water.

"It's getting dark," he murmured.

"I like it here. I like you."

He pursed his lips. The kiss was meant to be the end not the beginning. She had to see this wouldn't work.

She pressed her fingertips to his lips. "Don't argue. You're good in a crisis, you know. You were very wise about giving away the money."

"It's your money."

"It was less than fifty bucks. Not only will the magazine reimburse me, I'll get a great column out of it."

"Warning people against hitchhikers?"

She scrunched a handful of his shirt in her hand. "I'm going to tell them to always bring someone like you along."

"Don't put me on a pedestal, Evie."

"Like Elvis?" She tugged him toward the stairs and hopped up one. "You didn't let me finish. I can't tell you how much I admire anyone who's suffered what you've been through and has gone on to make a decent life for himself."

It looked pretty empty from where he stood. An apartment over a garage. A skill he could take with him anytime he wanted to pick up and move on. "I'm a mechanic. I don't have a college degree like you."

"You've got a good job, a boss who thinks the world of you, a woman who—" She paused.

He should have known she'd find the nerve to continue. Evie wasn't shy.

"You've got a woman who is very attracted to you and would like to know you better." Her blue eyes rested steadily on his.

The wind picked up, a hot gust from the south blowing strands of hair across her cheek. He chased them away, one finger at a time. Curling them behind her ear, he felt her shudder deep down when he caressed her earlobe. He rubbed it thoughtfully between his thumb and forefinger. "You've got this exaggerated picture of me."

Her arms locked around his neck, she leaned back for a better look. "I have twenty-twenty vision."

"I'm nobody's hero."

She brushed her lips lightly over his. "Be mine."

If she only knew how badly he wanted her. But he'd never been able to save anybody, not when it counted. Love fooled women. It made them take chances they shouldn't, make sacrifices nobody should make.

Holding her, tasting her tongue on his, he wanted to be the hero she saw in those hazy bedroom eyes.

The light was nearly gone. He stepped back. She searched his eyes in vain, fighting disappointment, waiting.

"Are we on the same floor?" he asked.

She hesitated then nodded.

He gripped her elbow, too rough, too rushed. "Let's go."

He hated misleading her. When she found out what he intended, maybe she'd hate *him*. She deserved more than he could ever give her. It was a lesson she needed to learn.

.

FIVE

Cole opened the bedroom window. Hot air scoured his bare chest. The curtains fluttered. He glanced at the bed. It would take more than a breeze to air out those rumpled sheets. A night of tossing and turning, alone, had set the wrinkles like bad concrete.

He picked up the receiver and punched her room number. She answered on the first ring. "It's almost nine," he said.

"What is this, wake-up call number three?"

"I thought you wanted to head out early."

"I don't recall mentioning it," she stated. Her laptop computer clicked in the background. She didn't mention the way he'd left her at her door without so much as a good-night kiss either. She didn't have to.

Slouching on the bed, he hauled his heels up onto the sheets and shoved a pillow behind his back. The back of his head thudded against the wall. He remembered the shock on her face, the flush of embarrassment and confusion he'd put there when he'd walked them back from the river, hustling her into the elevator as if he couldn't wait to get her to her room. Then he shut the door between them.

He owed her an apology. "Evie—"

She sensed where this was going before he even finished her name. "I've got work, Cole."

"I wanted to explain."

"What's to explain? He was a mixed up kid in need of food and shelter. Unfortunately for us, Brad, a.k.a. Luke, was also a snake—"

She must have shrugged while balancing the receiver on her shoulder. It landed soft as a sigh on the bed. Cole imagined other sighs taking place there. "It wasn't the kid I wanted to talk about."

"Later, okay? I've got two hundred and fifty words to go."

He set the receiver down. They had thousands of miles to go. He still loved her. That "my hero" stuff had unnerved him. He never wanted that pure undiscerning love directed his way. No man deserved it, and a million women had been hurt by it.

Love might have hog-tied him, but it was long past time to disillusion her.

"I was about to order lunch," he groused. "Eleven-thirty is kind of late to start."

"It's never too late to start," Evie sang out. Breezing around the trunk, she flung her suitcase inside. Let him fume; thanks to his hasty retreat the night before, she'd been spinning her wheels all morning. The article was a mangled rough draft. Her feelings were equally chaotic.

What had she done wrong? She hadn't blurted out "I love you" on the banks of the Mississippi, hadn't mentioned marriage or children or used that most dreaded of words *relationship.*And yet, standing outside her hotel-room door, he'd dropped her like a hot exhaust pipe.

She fished out her car keys and tossed them to him. "If you need munchies, the cooler is stocked with fruit and yogurt. As for me, I'm still working on my article. Thanks to a certain caller, I kept getting interrupted."

Not that it was all his fault. She'd tried calisthenics at dawn with a TV exercise program. After that she'd gotten caught up in a shame-and-blame talk show that made her feel even worse. *Men.*

The most confounding member of the species got behind the wheel. "If you want to get anywhere on this trip, we have to get going earlier," he said.

She muttered to her sideview mirror. "So Mr. We-Have-to-Stop becomes We-Ought-to-Start."

He gunned the engine and ground the gears. "Where to?"

Donning designer sunglasses, she tipped her nose in the air. "Kansas City is four hours west."

"And after that?"

She flipped open the laptop and started typing. "I haven't decided yet."

He looked left then right then peeled out of the garage. If she smelled burning rubber, she didn't comment.

❖————————❖

Tap tap tap. Evie's fingers clattered over the laptop keys. Cole noticed. She muttered aloud as she wrote—nothing he understood. For three hours she backspaced and erased, reading half sentences aloud, rewriting as she went. Every now and then she cursed, a woman's curses, *fudge, fiddlesticks,* and her favorite, *butternuts.*

Cole rolled his eyes. "It's like driving cross-country with Little Orphan Annie."

"Huh?" She scanned the rolling countryside as if a barn silo had spoken. When he said nothing, she went back to work.

Cole glared hard at the road. She seemed perfectly content wrestling with her opinion piece. He was ready to drink battery acid.

Tired explanations rumbled through his mind. He'd be bad for her. They had nothing in common. Look what happened anytime they got close. He'd kissed her on the banks of the Mississippi like a riverboat gambler saying good-bye to his one true love. Then he'd dumped her.

He deserved the cold shoulder. He deserved a royal chewing out. He got *tap, tap, tap,* a pounding headache, and a throbbing ache in his lower body that wouldn't quit.

He glanced across the car. Hot pink caught his eye. She wore a filmy silk shell. Every time she leaned forward, the shoulder dipped, the scooped neck threatened to reveal cleavage, and the wide armhole betrayed the swell of a breast. Her obliviousness to her own allure only made it worse.

He clenched the right-hand side of the wheel. He'd wanted her all night. Now she was inches away. He just had to reach for her. He could kiss her again, memorize the tang of her mouth, the satiny sheen of her lips. Instead he squinted at the grime on the edges of the windshield, the aerodynamic slope of the hood.

That worked for two miles. The woman never sat still. Dressed for a late-summer-day crossing the plains, she wore the pink shell, beige shorts, and sandals. The shoes came off and on as often as a blinking yellow light. She wedged her toes inside. She crossed her ankles. The laptop balanced on her bare thighs, the expanse of skin dusted with fine gold hair. Her cotton shorts were baggy, roomy, modest. His imagination made them bedroom material.

He flipped the air conditioner on high.

"It's freezing in here," she commented.

"It's seventy-five and humid."

"Outside maybe. It's an icebox in here."

Not from where he was sitting.

Her fingers hovered over the keys. She waited. He stared at the road. She leaned across a vent to shut it down.

Maybe she was right about the cold. The tiny nubs of her breasts came to life beneath the fabric of her sleeveless top. Cole gritted his teeth and opened the window. He balanced his elbow on the ledge. If he'd been a dog, he would've hung his whole head outside.

Clamping a pencil between her teeth, Evie ignored the inrush of air and went back to her article.

Cole returned to the subject of the previous night. "It was too early."

"I thought you said we left too late."

"It was too early for sex."

The pencil clattered over the keys and into her lap. Cole glared at it. She retrieved it, tugging the hem of her shorts an inch lower. "Who said anything about sex?"

"It was moving too fast."

"Like you?"

Eighty-five and rising. He eased off the gas. The bruise on his shin thrummed. He glanced into the rear-view mirror for flashing lights. "I didn't want us rushing into anything."

"I was *not* rushing," she declared hotly.

"We've known each other three days."

She huffed and tossed the pencil at her feet. Digging through a briefcase for diskettes, she slid one into the laptop and pressed a button. "What gets me is your tacit assumption that we were going to bed."

"That's where we were headed."

"We were heading for my room. People can talk."

"Sure. 'Do you prefer the bottom or the top?' "

She slammed the computer shut. "Of all the egotistical, Neanderthal male— Did it ever occur to you I might want to explore this attraction—"

"Explore," he said with a snort.

"There are chairs in my room. A settee—"

"Next to the king-size bed."

"That was in Knoxville."

"I remember."

She blinked when he held her gaze too long. "I had two double beds last night."

"I won't tell you what I had all night."

"A man and woman alone are not a sexual act about to happen."

He draped his wrist over the wheel and gave her an even longer look. "We are."

She squirmed in her seat, adjusting the shoulder strap so she could face him. "Despite what you think, fantasize, or otherwise dream, Cole Creek, there are early stages in a—a relationship." There, she'd said it. "We have chemistry, yes. That's no guarantee of consummation."

He worked his mouth into a tight line. "I don't think it's a good idea."

"I never said it was."

"I mean a relationship."

Despite every effort to keep her hopes from rising, Evie felt them plummet. The breath squeezed out of her lungs. "I wasn't throwing myself at you. A relationship can be anything: friendship, companionship."

He reached over, gripping her fingers with his. "I thought it'd get out of hand."

She hated it when men were "nice" about brushing her off. She disengaged her hand. "Fine. If that's all you want, just say so."

He hesitated, then leaned against his door. "If that's the way you want it."

"This is not all my fault."

"I never said it was."

"It might help if you didn't kiss me every time I turn around."

"I couldn't help it."

"That's a poor excuse."

"I want you."

But? There was always a but, Evie thought. Men who liked her but— Men who wanted a relationship but— He said he wanted her but—

"We aren't right for each other," he concluded.

She threw up her hands. "How would you know if we never get to know each other?"

"Because I—" He stopped there, swinging out to pass a tanker truck.

"Because you what?"

What could he tell her? That he loved her? That there was nothing halfway about his feelings for her? That he'd been picturing her in his apartment, his bed, out of those clothes, in them, it didn't matter. "I didn't want it going too far." It had already gone further than he'd ever allowed himself to go. He held out little hope for getting back his heart when this trip was done.

"I *am* capable of saying no," she muttered.

He slanted his hips forward, his knee bumping the underside of the steering wheel. "I don't know about that." Settling his elbow on the seat back between them, he shot her a look. "Want to prove it?" He took his foot off the gas.

Evie glanced rapidly behind them. There were few cars on the road. Theirs rapidly slowed. Cole angled it toward the shoulder. The tires rumbled on rough pavement, reminding her of the risky rumble in his voice.

"I can pull off, Evie, anytime you say. We could find a turnoff, a country road. You name it. We'll 'explore' this to your heart's content." He ran the backs of his fingers down her bare arm.

Her gaze darted to the speedometer, her heart racing. "You're going too slow."

"Want me to speed up?"

She swept his fingers off her arm.

"You tell me you can handle this. I'm telling you it's going to get out of control unless one of us says stop."

"And that's you, of course," she said.

"Something ignites when I'm around you. Discussing it, in a room with a bed, would be like tossing a lit match on gasoline."

Folding her arms securely across her chest, she nodded at a billboard. "Speaking of gas."

"There's enough to get us to Kansas City. Just. Of course, if you want me to stop, all you have to do is say so."

As far as she was concerned, they'd barely gotten started. In three short days she'd learned about his painful background, watched him risk his life for her purse, caught glimpses of his sly humor and fundamental decency. She'd begun to care for him.

"Evie? Do you want to stop?"

She swallowed the lump in her throat. "We'd better keep going. I told Mike I'd be there by five."

"Who's Mike?"

Chin in the air, she wasn't about to fill him in.

Fist churning around the wheel, Cole didn't ask.

"I just don't get this idea that we can't have a relationship."

Evie's frustrated pronouncement came forty minutes later on the outskirts of Kansas City. She couldn't have picked a worse time. Five lanes of rush-hour traffic doing seventy on every side, Cole tried to decipher the exits beneath flapping orange detour signs. A flashing arrow on the back of a construction truck narrowed the road to two merged lanes.

"Who's to say a relationship can't be simple friendship? Cole?"

"What?"

"You're not listening to me."

How could he when the car beside him refused to let him merge left? They had a thousand yards before this lane ended. "It's not you, it's me."

"I see." Clearly, she'd heard that one before.

He'd been thinking it for the last hour—ever since she'd slid her hand out of his with that shamed expression. "You want to know what did it?"

"I'm sure you'll tell me."

"You calling me a hero. I'm nobody's hero, Evie."

"You chased down that mugger as if you were Clint Eastwood."

"It was stupid and dangerous. You cornering him in the alley wasn't too swift either."

"Apparently it was more forgivable than kissing you 'thank you.' You've been running ever since."

He grimaced. "I am not running. I just don't want you falling in love with me, okay?" He knew from recent experience how frustrating that emotion could be. One fool in love was plenty.

He peered at the upcoming exit. Had he missed it? Honking at a road-hog Winnebago, he sped beyond it, riding dangerously close to a Toyota's back bumper. Evie had gone completely silent. He glanced over.

She pounced. "I can't believe you just said that!"

He stared at a mile of slow-moving brake lights. "I

don't want any woman getting so head over heels in love with me, she doesn't see the real man. That's all I meant."

Her mouth hung open as she dragged in an outraged squeak. "Of all the egotistical, pigheaded, cockamamie, zipper-thinking idiocy."

"Evie."

"You think after one night with you, I'd be head over heels in love!"

One day with her and he'd been.

She unlatched her seat belt. Always a bad sign. Swinging around, she got in position to give him what for. "Listen you, I do *not* throw myself into relationships. I'd rather die than make that mistake again. Just because I called you my hero—"

"Doesn't mean you meant it?"

A honking horn evoked a short curse from him and a swift change of lanes.

She swayed back into her seat. "You *were* a hero. That doesn't mean I was teetering on the edge of eternal love! Or sex. I thought we might explore the next stage of this relationship. *If* there was going to be one, which obviously there isn't."

"Then it was the adrenaline talking."

"You said it!"

Disgusted, Evie folded her arms and clamped her legs at the knees. Kansas City's downtown loomed in the distance. She scowled at it as they crept along. Peering out the side window, she wondered how anyone who'd just won an argument could feel so defeated.

She'd smiled up at him with that dewy-eyed hero-worship line, then kissed him for all she was worth.

When would she ever learn? She shouldn't express her feelings so openly, so soon. Love wasn't spontaneous. It required discretion, tact, fine tuning.

But she'd been so sure he wanted to kiss her, the way he held her, the tender, urgent way his mouth had opened and drawn her in. He'd put his coat around her shoulders so protectively—

And she'd read way too much into it. As usual.

She stifled a groan. Creeping along with the traffic, he closed his window against the exhaust fumes. Cold musty air hissed out of the air conditioner. Evie folded her arms.

He didn't want her loving him. He'd come right out and said so. What more did she need, an EPA sticker? An Underwriters Laboratories label? A skull and crossbones that read DANGER, THIS MAN HAZARDOUS TO YOUR HEALTH?

She fixed her gaze on a distant office tower. "I promised Mike I'd fax my article by five-thirty."

"So he's your editor?"

"Don't sound so relieved. He'll be my ex-editor if I don't get this article in. All I need is a modem and a fax. There, the Blue Ridge Mall. Try that."

"I've been looking for an exit."

She had the rotten feeling he'd already taken it.

She pulled Mike's next assignment from the fax machine and marveled. *Tell us more about the car*, her boss requested. It needed washing. It ran. It got them where they were going.

But where were they going?

She tossed the fax in a folder. Cars were the least of her worries.

She stalked around the Conquest's driver's side.

"We could get a couple hot dogs and take in a game," Cole suggested. "Kauffman Stadium's just down the road."

"So?"

"Kansas City Royals. Two games out. Two weeks left in the season."

The image of sitting beside him while happy people cheered and shouted and did the Wave, made her suddenly feel like crying. "We wouldn't get out until late."

"We can stay in KC tonight."

And have a strained dinner in some hotel restaurant? No thanks. "I want to make Wichita tonight."

Cole sighed. "If it was anything I said . . ."

"You've made your feelings perfectly clear." And she'd made the usual mistakes, revealing her feelings too fast, plunging in. "I want to keep going."

Dead silent, he reached for the radio and turned on the instantly recognizable hubbub of a stadium crowd in between pitches. "Must be a doubleheader. At least we can listen."

In her typical heart-on-her-sleeve fashion, Evie knew she'd said too much already.

In the sunny morning light, Fiona picked up her favorite crystal. She'd been looking for answers, clues, auras. Where she expected a prism of color, she got images of chaos, swirling and muddy. Something very odd was going on.

It was that woman in Ohio. But Eve wasn't in Ohio—

of that Fiona was sure. And the man in question. He was in . . . Kansas? Iowa? One of those middle states.

Fiona shook her head; this got worse and worse. Perhaps she'd eaten something spicy before the show. Maybe her change of life was interfering with her insight.

She sighed and put the crystal down. Time to call Austin in the Evening *and press him for a return visit. She had an eerie feeling this woman and her noncommittal man were headed for trouble. Big trouble. The kind that tore people apart.*

Or forged them together for life.

"Idiot. The flaws in their logic, I swear. What good would tariffs do for trade with Canada? Canada's our friend!"

Evie had taken the wheel first thing the next morning as they left Wichita. Arguing with a talk-radio disc jockey, she swiveled to look over her shoulder as she scooted in and out of traffic.

"What about some music?" Cole offered.

"I like talk radio. It gives you someone to talk to."

"So you can argue with thin air?"

"So? If someone we both know would talk a little more, I wouldn't have to."

"We're not starting that again."

"Tariffs on Canadian goods are counterproductive. What do you think?"

Cole thought there was enough tension between them without bringing Canada into it. He reached over the backseat for her folder of maps. Removing them one by one, he refolded them properly and stowed them alphabetically. Next he went to work on her collection of tapes.

"Stop that."

"You shouldn't have to take your eye off the road to find what you want."

"I had them organized."

"Paul Simon beside U2? *Gypsy* next to *The Barber of Seville*?"

"So I'm eclectic."

"It'll only take a minute."

"Give me the Gershwin."

"Not Gershwin," he muttered.

She imperiously held out her hand. "If you don't want to listen to politics . . ."

"We've heard Gershwin twice."

She fumbled through the tapes and came up with another. After she poked it into the tapedeck, the strains of "Wichita Lineman" filled the car.

"Perfect." She hummed along, settling in for the drive. Eventually the road narrowed to two lanes. Evie watched for an upcoming mile marker. "Dodge City!" She hauled herself forward, gripping the wheel.

"What about it?"

"This isn't the way to Texas! We're on the wrong road."

"You took it straight out of Wichita."

"But I wanted to head south through Oklahoma to Fort Worth."

"You never told me."

Everything she'd told him so far had come out revealing and wrong. "Damn." She reached for the map. He got it for her.

"Now where did you want to go?"

She frowned, as if focusing harder would make the road widen. "This isn't a major freeway."

"You didn't notice? It's been two lanes for thirty miles."

"I thought we were entering Oklahoma. It's approximately one hundred miles south of Wichita. This—"

"This is one hundred miles *west*."

"But I don't want to be here," she wailed.

"You think I like it?"

"Don't start, Creek."

"I didn't mean it personally."

"Just tell me how to get back on I-35."

"It's too late. Besides, if we aren't going anywhere in particular, Dodge City's as good as anything."

"Fine."

"Fine."

"Fine." She was collecting more fines than a speed trap. "Give me that." She plastered the Kansas map to the wheel. Reading and speeding, she veered left. A driver honked. She spit out a choice epithet. It wasn't *butternuts*. "Where's Oklahoma?"

"South of here."

"I mean the map."

He handed over Oklahoma.

She unfolded it on top of Kansas and started reading. "From Dodge we'll angle down to Liberal then south to Guymon. Once we cross into Texas, we'll head straight south to—where's Texas?"

"South of here—"

Her scowl cut his smart remark in two. He handed

her the map. She'd practically papered the windshield with it.

"Think we got enough paper floating around?" he asked.

Texas was too big for one side of the map. She tried flipping it to the Panhandle side. Oklahoma curled onto her lap. Kansas crinkled backward. She let out a frustrated squeak and handed the crackling mass to Cole. "We'll find Amarillo when we get there."

"If we get there."

"I've had about enough with the sarcasm."

"Sorry."

Too wired to relax, she fiddled with the radio knobs. "Where are my tapes?"

"Don't tell me, let me guess. 'Amarillo by Morning,' George Strait."

"What's wrong with George Strait?"

"I didn't know we were on a Musical Mystery Tour. 'Walking in Memphis,' 'Graceland,' 'Kansas City.' When we get to California it'll be 'Do You Know the Way to San Jose?' and 'I Left My Heart in San Francisco.' "

"You forgot 'I Love L.A.' by Randy Newman."

"I take it you didn't."

Without cracking a smile, he'd teased her out of her snippy mood. She tossed him a look. "We've got to cross 'Rocky Mountain High' first. And 'Rocky Mountain Way.' "

He groaned.

"I thought I'd program music for every change of scenery. Keep things from getting dull."

It'd never be that between the two of them. Cole scanned the flat terrain. "Looks like Kansas to me."

Energized by the unforeseen change of plan, Evie sat up straight. "We'll have lunch in Dodge then head south. After we cross the Oklahoma Panhandle, we'll head down into Texas."

" 'The Yellow Rose of . . . '?"

She grinned entirely against her will. "We'll be in Amarillo by *evening.*"

Glancing in her rearview mirror, she was suddenly aware of Cole's gaze resting on her. Her skin colored just enough to send a breath of heat over her cheeks. She slanted a look his way to confirm what her senses told her.

He kept looking, studying her with a thousand-mile gaze that wasn't going anywhere, a lazy leisurely tour along her profile.

She drew a strand of hair behind her ear. Confronting her fears was one thing. She'd gotten in more trouble than she cared to admit fessing up to her desires. All the same, she couldn't resist. "What?"

"Just thinking of Amarillo."

"Have you ever been there?"

He shook his head. "I was picturing another hotel."

And another kiss? she thought, kneading the steering wheel with her fist. "I'm sorry I've been so tense this morning."

"Not enough sleep?"

Too many dreams. "You're right about our not getting involved. Not that I'm saying we would have had sex." Her imperious, flat-out, no-way gesture made him smile. "It'd only complicate things. This is a very tight space."

He turned his chin toward the backseat, as if imagining how tight it could get. "Mm-hmm."

She squirmed in the contour seat. Its back molded her hips a tad too intimately. "It's me. I tend to go overboard. Don't ask why."

He quietly asked who.

She should have known it then, should have suspected. He cared more than he let on. But suspecting was one step from wishing. She didn't want to read anything into his long silences. The only declarations he'd come right out and made concerned stopping. As her friend Shelly said, sometimes a hungry look just meant a man hadn't eaten in a while.

She shook her head at her own foolishness. She'd been in such a hurry to get out of Wichita, so addled by her wrong turn. She didn't want to take another. Which was why she was especially careful when he asked where she got the idea she went overboard.

"You seem honest, sure," he added. "Nothing wrong with that."

"According to my friends there is."

"Close friends?"

"Girlfriends, boyfriends. *Ex*-boyfriends. I expect too much."

"Is that a sin?"

"It's like a product. If something's wrong, you don't put up with it, you send it to the manufacturer, complain to the seller, get it replaced, repaired."

An amused grin crinkled the skin around his eyes.

She tore her gaze away and focused on the endless gray ribbon of road.

"Relationships don't come with a warranty," he pointed out.

"If things aren't moving along, I see nothing wrong with confronting them, discussing what's happening, fixing what's wrong."

"And the men you knew didn't want to be fixed?"

"Careful how you put that. One of them was a veterinarian."

He laughed.

She reached for the cola she'd set in the cup holder beneath the radio. "It's like buying a new car. You don't sit in the parking lot, you take it out on the road. Up hills, around corners. See what it can do."

"All on the first day?"

She chewed briefly on her straw. "See? I do do too much."

"On the first day? A man might get the wrong impression."

"I get excited about possibilities. That doesn't mean I'm desperate. Men confuse the two. They can't deal with intense. With up-front."

"Some men can't."

It was his sleepy tone, his low rumbling murmur that refused to judge, that let her leap in to fill in the blanks. A gang of motorcycles passed them going the other way.

"I guess it's a two-way street," she admitted. "Maybe I am to blame."

And maybe the men who'd dumped her were idiots. Cole watched her mouth form a tiny O around her straw, the pull of her cheeks hollowing as she sucked on her cola. "Some man might come along who likes those qualities," he suggested. And Cole, when he heard about it back in the garage in Dearborn, would eat his heart out.

He closed a fist around a can of iced tea from her cooler.

She waved her drink for emphasis. "I've been trying to tone it down."

And cool down their attraction by telling him all the ways she'd screwed up as a woman. Cole figured that much. He let her chatter on, watching the rare hint of vulnerability shadow her eyes, and hating himself for letting it linger.

She shoved her cola in the flimsy fold-down cup holder. "The upshot of all this is, I haven't thrown myself at you," she declared with suitable finality. A mile marker zipped by. "Have I?"

Head leaning against the headrest, eyes restlessly taking in the unchanging landscape, Cole shook his head. "I'm still here."

"True. But you would tell me if I was being too forward."

"Sure." It was the quality he'd fallen in love with first. He flashed back to that first morning, the outstretched hand, her willingness to step forward. Next on his list was her smile, her face, her body. Her honesty was third. She clicked with him, like a key in a lock, opening one door after another.

He detoured around her question. "Doesn't seem like three days, does it?"

She took a deep breath and sighed. "Hardly. That's

the thing about dates. Most men you meet, you go to dinner or a movie, sit in the dark, watch an action picture. A week later you do it again. Small talk about work, family. He's got a business trip, so it's two weeks before the next date. Then there's the first kiss."

From a near doze to a face-hardened frown, Cole didn't like the path she was taking. He yanked on his shoulder belt and sat up.

"You don't learn that much about a man," Evie said, "not in the first couple weeks. Maybe that's why I try too hard; I want to know it all, up-front."

He cleared his throat. "Nothing wrong with that. You don't want to get trapped in something you never saw coming."

"But look at us. After three days I feel I know you more than men I've dated for months."

"Is that why we keep getting in trouble?"

She turned a scolding, bemused look his way. "A few kisses are hardly trouble."

Tell it to his lower body.

"I was talking about how well we know each other. Comparatively. Now, take Christopher, he was so distant. I dated him for two years and never felt—"

Cole didn't want to hear it. He wasn't a buddy, he wasn't a girlfriend. He couldn't stop her. Against all his better judgment, all his feeble attempts to drive her off, she kept walking right back into his heart, fearlessly revealing her faults, foibles, yearnings, mistakes.

His mother would have never admitted a fault to her husband; the price she would have paid in ridicule, disdain, and sheer punishment was too high. Evie expected to be accepted, to be listened to.

Cole balanced his elbow on the window ledge and leaned his mouth against his fist, the better to hide a frustrated sigh. How the hell did she expect him to resist her?

Coming to the end of her short list of faults, she jolted him back to attention with her conclusion. "What bothers me is that you made up your mind about us before we even gave it a shot."

"You said yourself, it would get complicated."

"But we can be friends."

Not the way he felt. He wanted that hope, that optimism—all the while distrusting it. He wanted that enthusiasm, to hold that spirit in his arms and let it flood into him, reviving a heart as shriveled as the stalks of corn lining the road.

"There's a station up ahead," he said. "We should stop."

She tried to tease him out of his sudden mood. "We've done nothing *but* stop."

He wasn't laughing.

SIX

His silence filled the car as she pulled into the small station. She angled the car around the lone self-serve pump. A weathered bench rested outside a tiny store, its desolate vantage point populated by two men in overalls. Hot air blew dust across their boots. "Howdy," one said.

Getting out of the car, Evie smiled. "Hi." A humid breeze billowed her skirt. She wore a flimsy summer sundress, straps crisscrossing in the back. The assessing gazes of the men were more appreciative than ogling. She took it as a compliment.

Cole said nothing. She listened to his door open and shut. As he passed her the wind caught her skirt, buffeting his legs.

She teased his thoughtful frown. "Howdy."

He yanked a blue paper towel from a dispenser.

"Mighty friendly 'round these parts," she murmured.

He turned on his heel and walked right up to her. Their bodies balanced inches apart.

She caught her breath. His gaze fell to the curve of her neck, the bare triangle of skin where the straps crossed her shoulder. The wind ravished her hair. She lifted her hand to hold it back. Slowly her palm slid downward over the sensitive flesh on the side of her neck, that patch of freckled skin. She didn't know whether she wanted to hide it from his scouring glance or touch it, imagining his touch, his searing kiss.

"I need in," he said.

Her mouth went dry. "Pardon me?"

He touched her elbow.

Startled, she stepped to her left. He hauled open the door and leaned inside to pop the hood.

Evie deflated like a punctured tire.

Cole shut the door with an airless thud. She followed him around the front of the car. "You don't have to pump gas every time we stop," she said. "I am capable."

"Capable of saying no?"

She lowered her voice. "What is it with you? I said we could be friends. I thought you agreed."

"It'll never work. Watch your fingers."

She took her hand off the fender as he hoisted the hood. Wrenching the radiator cap to the left, he let a plume of steam escape.

Evie glared at his determined, stony face. She considered retreating to the passenger seat. But the Conquest's tan leather upholstery looked hot and sticky. Her legs tingled, restless, cramped, in need of a stretch. She arched her back, fingers spread on her hips.

Cole stooped to refill the windshield-wiper fluid.

"Cole, I'm sorry if I've done anything forward. I do tend to rush into relationships, but to tell you the truth, I'm sick and tired of apologizing for liking you."

He grunted and wiped a grease smudge off the champagne-colored paint with the towel.

She slapped the fiberglass fender. "We have to get along. We're partners here. If you're not comfortable, we can set limits."

He straightened, his blue eyes lasering into hers. "Then we're sunk already."

"How?"

His gaze skimmed from her billowing hair to the sheen of pink in her cheeks. She felt the heat well in her, spreading across her chest, melting through her. She wanted to shift from foot to foot, to ease the nagging languid feeling weighing her down, the zinging electric current that told her something else was going on here. "If I can stick to limits, you can."

He glared at the engine. "I don't feel about you the way you feel about me."

Embarrassment straightened her spine. "I got that part, Creek. As I said, I have no intention of throwing myself at you."

"You're not the one I'm worried about."

He didn't care about her feelings. He'd made that perfectly clear. Message received.

And, with all due respect, thoroughly ignored. If he didn't want to get involved, why did he look so damn lonely? Every time he backed off from a kiss, he squared his shoulders like a man going to his own execution. Or a hitchhiker sticking his thumb out as he began a thousand-mile journey.

She'd never accept a manufacturer's claims regarding a new product. How could she sit back and accept Cole's claim that he wasn't interested? Especially when experience kept proving him wrong? There was something he wasn't saying.

Of course, that could be her wishful thinking kicking in, her innate ability to fill in other people's blanks. She tested this out for herself. She spread her hands on the warm fender. "Okay, Mr. Mechanic, tell me how this works."

"It's an engine."

"I have an expert on staff; I should learn something new. Tell me what's going on here."

"I wish I knew," he muttered.

"What was that?"

He wiped his hands on the towel.

Evie resorted to the lowest tactic she could think of; male pride. "Mike says 'tell us more about the car.' Personally I think that would be deadly dull—"

"There's a lot your readers should know. This make has a lot of innovations." Cole relayed a spate of information that would presumably satisfy her editor. "On the other hand," he added, "I don't like the way she's torquing, the idle's set too high, and the mileage is less than optimal."

"That may be because it's new."

"It can do better. Part of that's the idle." He stared at the engine block.

"Can you fix it?"

"If I set it too low, the engine could stall out."

"Mm." She leaned in closer, her shoulder nearly touching his. "Did I ever tell you about the time my car stalled on the railroad tracks and that train came around the bend . . . ? Never mind. You were saying?"

His shoulders tensed and his mouth drew into a fine line.

Her hip bumped his slightly.

"This would be hell to work on," he said gruffly. He pointed a finger at a nest of wires. "It'd cost an hour of labor just getting to it."

"Why would you have to do that?"

"To get to the carb."

"Ah," she murmured wisely. "Carbohydrates."

He used the rag to fiddle with another cap. "From a consumer standpoint, there's not a lot a do-it-your-selfer could do."

"And it's so hard finding good help nowadays." She sighed.

A vein throbbed in his neck. "The choke is set by computer; the fuel injection needs to be regulated by an expert, and the timing belt's impossible to reach. Replacing a headlight requires removing the entire grille. They do that a lot nowadays. Then there's the fiberglass."

He said it as if he'd just swallowed some. She eased in closer, her windblown skirt flirting with his legs once more. "Is that bad?"

"It's nice if you don't like rust. But one fender bender and the whole thing needs replacing."

Like the two of them? One wrong move and their tenuous connection stalled out. The hunger she'd glimpsed in him died and her jokes went up in smoke. "I'll get my notebook and write this down," she muttered.

She flounced around to the passenger side and sank into her seat. Rifling through the glove box, she found her notebooks—color-coordinated and alphabetized during his map-folding mania outside Kansas City.

A flash of color swung by the window—his shirt. She watched his hand clench around the handle as he slid the gas nozzle into the tank. Deciding the whole thing was too symbolic, she went back to her notes. She jumped when a sodden squeegee slapped her side window. Cole swiped it clean in two strokes. Lavishing the same attention on the windshield, he pressed his chest against it.

Evie watched the expansion and contraction of his chest muscles, the tease of curling gold hair where he'd unbuttoned the top two buttons on his plaid shirt. Unbelted jeans clung to his lean waist.

The pump dinged. In the side mirror's tiny frame, she watched his shoulder blades ripple as he twisted to put the nozzle back. His shirt was badly wrinkled, plastered to his back from sitting so long. She wanted to peel it off him.

She closed her eyes and rested her head against the headrest. A trickle of perspiration slithered beneath her breast, soaking into the fabric at her waist. Her thighs grew damp everywhere they touched. My, but cars got hot sitting in the sun, she thought. You couldn't warn people often enough about leaving dogs and unattended children in a closed car. . . .

The driver's door swung open. A gust of air carried

in the musky scent of his skin. Evie sat up, realizing with a guilty flush that she'd been inhaling his scent on the headrest. His shape loomed over her. Something clicked.

He pulled his mileage and maintenance notebook from the glove box. Then he was gone. The closed door created an air-lock thud.

Evie pulled her hair back from her face. She tried to keep her thoughts on the trip, the cornfields all around them, the endless blue sky. Through the slit in the hood, she watched him fiddle with the engine once more. As if frustrated by something, he leaned both hands on the fender. Tapering fingers curved over it, gripping, tensing. Powerful, elegant, callused, clean. She wondered how those hands would feel molding a woman's breast. Full, overly sensitive breasts.

His jeans were sleek and faded, worn to a buttery softness. A threadbare patch on his thigh threatened to reveal tanned skin. Along his zipper the denim had faded nearly white.

Her mouth was bone-dry, her body restless, her lungs clogged with stuffy air. Evie chided herself for pretending this was about wrists and worn denim. She'd spent five minutes staring straight at his crotch.

Irritated with herself, agitated by the time he'd wasted petting and coddling that mass of machinery, she got out. The store should have some lemonade or iced tea. It might quench her thirst. She doubted it would do anything for this gnawing hunger.

◆──────────◆

She came at him, two cans of iced tea clutched in her hands. Beads of moisture glittered down their silver sides. A sheen of moisture glistened on her forehead. "Want one?"

Time slowed down. Heat waves rose from the pavement. She waded through it, a siren come to life. The heels of her sandals tocked against the asphalt. That drew his eyes to her legs, the way her dress slithered in and out between them.

He'd been hiding, letting the engine's heat waves leach this ragged longing out of his system. It worked —until she'd extended that can.

He dragged his arm across his upper lip and accepted. "Thanks."

"You looked like you could use some."

He swallowed. "I'm trying to adjust this." Adjust *to* it was more like it. He'd kept the women in his life on the fringes—companions, dates. She'd walked into his life and changed everything.

He wondered if his mother had felt that way about his father.

He tasted tar and exhaust. He downed half the tea in one gulp. A breath of air brought a hint of her scent his way. He drowned it with another gulp. Setting the can down, he went back to fixing things that weren't broken. He wanted to keep them that way.

She watched him, standing too close. His fist clenched around a pair of pliers. His fingers danced along something hot. He hissed at the pain.

She pursed her lips, ready to kiss it and make it better.

That'd only make it worse.

He straightened and wiped his hands on a rag. "That's about all I can do for now."

"Did it help?"

Killing time would kill the longing. Since day one it had lurked in the back of his mind, throbbing through his dreams, sizzling beneath his skin. "There's something you should know."

She dabbed her lips with the back of her wrist. "What is it?"

"How to check the oil."

For a minute she didn't move. Her pale throat rippled as she swallowed another sip of tea. "All right. Show me." She took a spot at the front of the car and leaned in.

She tried concentrating, watching the crinkly brown hair on his forearm as he reached for the dipstick, the flexing tendons on the underside of his wrist as he turned it over and showed her the markings.

"This is full, a quart low, half a quart, et cetera."

"Got it."

"You put this here."

The flat metal stick slid into the dark hole, its edge scraping the entrance. The hairs on her neck stood on end. She shivered despite the heat.

Cole slowly withdrew the stick. He held a paper towel under it. "You can see where the oil is."

A thin honeylike liquid coated the stick. As they watched, a gold drop collected at the end, then fell on the engine. Something burned. Something hissed. A drop of perspiration trickled the length of her spine.

Evie nodded. Hair stuck to the back of her neck in coiled tendrils. She pulled it up, balancing it on the back of her head, hoping the air would cool her off. The motion pulled the fabric of her dress tighter across her breasts, easing the ache collecting there.

Cole slid the stick back into the hole. He spent a long moment staring at the engine, then wiped his hands on a second towel. "Anything else you wanted to know?"

Denying her needy heart only sent her emotions in another direction—pure lust. His insistence on keeping her at a distance made her want him more. She told herself the heat made it worse, but that wouldn't explain her wanting him that first night in Knoxville or St. Louis or every mile they'd shared in this too-small sedan.

She peered at the lines around his eyes, the rigid set of his jaw. Why wouldn't he let her in? Because he didn't want her loving him? Who on earth had so much love they could turn away more?

And who said anything about love? her conscience asked.

She dropped her arm, the hair instantly gluing itself to her damp skin. "Anything else I want to know," she mused.

"Master mechanic, at your service." But afraid to look at her.

She wondered briefly if his demonstration had been as suggestive to him as to her. Even the possibility added heat to her overheated skin. "Do I have to check the oil every time we stop?"

"Once a week when she's new. Once a month after that. Use a quick-change place."

"I can do it myself."

"It's a dirty job."

"Somebody's got to do it." If he didn't touch her soon, she'd scream.

"Hard to imagine you under a car with an oil pan."

"Yeah?" She pictured him instantly and vividly, dollying out from under a car, flat on his back, T-shirt dirty, jeans stretched taut across his hips. "Why does she need it so often?"

He looked at her a long moment, a crooked brow questioning her use of the word *she*. "Cars need lubrication."

She took a slow breath of heat-filled air. "Do they?"

"When gas enters the engine it's ignited by the spark plugs. They propel the pistons into the cylinders. It creates a pumping motion."

"Pumping."

"If the cylinders aren't lubricated, you get friction. Friction leads to heat."

"I'll bet it does."

"Next thing you know—"

Her eyes met his. "Yes?"

His Adam's apple bobbed. His lips were dry, full, wary. "When that happens, a red light comes on. When you see that, stop immediately."

She gripped the can to her chest, its cold surface sending shock waves through her skin. "Couldn't we coast awhile?"

"Better to deal with it right away."

"Get off the road."

"Or add oil."

Lubrication wasn't the problem. Her knees felt

weak. A watery honeyed feeling flowed through her, gathering at the juncture of her thighs.

He reached for his back pocket. "I'll get the bill."

Her eyes strayed downward when he flipped open his wallet. The circular bulge beside his credit cards looked suggestively familiar. She wondered how long he'd carried that condom. Was it for her or anyone who came along? Maybe he was as casual about sexual encounters as she was methodical. She watched him walk toward the store.

"When I come back, I'll drive," he announced.

She shrugged. He'd been driving her wild for twenty minutes. Why stop now?

He strode out of the store. Retrieving his warm iced tea from the fender, he finished it off, crushed the can, then tossed it in an open barrel. The metal rang as they pulled away.

Who was he kidding? Cole wondered blackly. He'd kissed her once, he'd do it again. He'd pretend it was wrong, then he'd be back wanting more. He was in love with her.

And making her crazy in the process. One look, one innocent conversation about internal combustion and the heat rose like water dancing on a griddle. The texture of the air changed. His throat grew parched and his lungs scratchy. His jeans bound tight, his body throbbed, and his pulse rattled worse than a Model T.

What's worse, she knew it. He saw it in those expressive blue eyes, the worry, the anticipation, the hope. It killed him not to touch her. His heart had gone out to her the first time they met. It was only a matter of time before his body followed.

They arrived in Dodge around one o'clock and went immediately to a tourist spot where "the Old West comes alive."

The two-block section of Hollywood facades featured wooden sidewalks, horses tied to rails, various saloons with swinging doors and tinkling pianos. The tourist crowds had been thinned by the recent start of the school year. However, Evie found them the most interesting part of the exhibit. "Why people buy things has always fascinated me."

Cole's mouth curved in a bemused grin as she slunk into a store filled with tacky trinkets, "Welcome to Dodge" ashtrays, and Aces 'n' Eights playing cards. She viewed the customers from a corner like an anthropologist studying some exotic species. "Look at all these men."

"They look normal enough to me."

"They're all wearing cowboy hats. It's like Colonial Williamsburg or Greenfield Village. Even the customers are in costume."

"Men wear cowboy hats in this part of the country."

"Did you wear one in Montana?"

"Didn't stop until a few years ago. Felt naked without it."

She wished he hadn't said that. Since their stop at the gas station, she'd been trying to think cooling thoughts.

He pulled a Stetson off the rack. Feet planted, hips slanted, he stood before a full-length mirror and settled the hat on his head. Folding the brim just so, he slanted it over one eye. "How's that, ma'am?"

It took her breath away.

She strode outside to the weathered plank sidewalk. Inhaling the smell of manure and dirt streets, she closed her eyes tight and listened to the clip-clop of horses, the squeak of leather harnesses, the creak of a Wells Fargo coach rattling by, and the chatter of tourists. The scent of ice cream wafted under her nose. She opened her eyes.

"You looked like you could use something cool."

"How'd you guess?" She gripped the cone with a trembling hand. His gaze rested on her like a brand. "Mm, vanilla. My favorite."

"Evie?"

"What?" She glanced up reluctantly.

A dashing cowboy grinned at her from the shadows beneath his hat brim. "That's chocolate."

Her heart stuttered to a halt. She licked the creamy coolness off her upper lip. She tasted nothing but him. The arid dusty smell of him blocked out all other senses. His shadow blocked out the sun.

He swept his hat off and curved his arm around her waist. He bent his head closer.

"Please don't," she begged.

"What trouble can we get into here? In broad daylight?"

"Too much."

"There's no such thing as too much."

He kissed her. In a sense, he'd been doing it all along. His lips had danced lightly over hers as he talked, making her crazy, stoking her longing.

She pressed her mouth to his, pleading for more. The taste of his tongue scalded hers.

"Ooh, take a picture, take a picture," someone squealed.

Like a mosquito's distant buzz, the sound was annoying but nothing Evie had to deal with. Not yet. Her knees melted like the ice cream in her cone. Sticky liquid trickled over her fingers.

His lips molded to her mouth; his lower body angled forward. She stepped into his embrace, her tongue cradling his, pulsing like the blood flowing thickly through their veins.

She ran her hand up his back. Every sinew responded. Brazenly, she looped a finger through a belt loop and tugged him closer. He came willingly, his knee subtly parting hers. Her arm got pinned between them. Neither noticed.

She gasped at the sudden shock of icy cold. The cone was melting rapidly in the late-summer heat. A chocolate-colored teardrop slid lazily down her chest, heading for the sultry sweet spot between her breasts. She tried to extricate her arm.

Cole eased his grip. He looked down. For a heart-hammering moment she knew he wanted to lick it off. Instead he reached for her wrist and brought it to his lips. He kissed her rapid pulse first, then the base of her palm, then her thumb. His tongue darted between her fingers, lapping up the ice cream that had dribbled there.

A woman with a camera shooed her children away. Gunslingers and shoot-outs were one thing. Lovers were something children needed to be protected from.

Cole reached for the cone. He licked it hungrily, forming his mouth over the top as if it were a breast and a cream-covered nipple.

Eyes shut, he tilted his head back and savored the taste on his tongue. When he opened his eyes, Evie was staring. "Did that cool you off?"

"You know it didn't." Her voice was as hoarse and ragged as an old barn blanket.

His wasn't much better. "Still hot?"

"On fire."

"There's got to be someplace we can go."

"Don't play at this."

Her plea hit him like a whiplash. He combed his fingers through her hair. "You think I'm playing?"

"One minute you want me to stop, the next—"

"It's me who needs stopping. I want you."

She drew in a shaky breath.

He'd finally said it. Part of it. He whipped off his hat and dragged a sleeve across the band of sweat on his forehead. He found himself twisting the hat in his hands like an aw-shucks cowboy in some corny Western. He squinted at the street. It had gotten real quiet.

Outside the Dodge City Bank, a black-hatted outlaw stepped into the center of the road. A tin star glinted off the sheriff's leather vest. The audience held their collective breath as the men took their places.

Evie stared into Cole's eyes. "I want you too," she said.

"Then let's get the hell out of Dodge." He gripped her elbow and turned her toward the parking lot. Behind them shots rang out. The crowd cheered. They hardly noticed.

SEVEN

They sat silent and stiff for twenty minutes, driving until they found the 54 junction and turned south into Oklahoma.

Evie folded the maps, tossing the mess onto the backseat. Cole took her hand. Twining his fingers through hers wasn't enough. He kissed her hand, her palm, gnawing on her soft skin.

She'd never put her seat belt on. One foot curled under her. Her skirt dipped between her parted thighs. When he kissed her wrist she turned toward him, substituting her other hand so she could run the free one through his hair.

He groaned and pressed his head to the headrest. She found his neck, kneading it. A womanly smile curved her lips each time he moaned and tilted his head for more.

"Amarillo's a few hours yet," she said.

"We'll get there by dinner."

Neither expected to eat.

She scooted over. "Maybe I can make driving easier."

He groaned when her fingers dug into the tension in his collarbone. "Who said we have to drive?"

She glanced shyly at the rural expanse. "Not many places to pull over."

"There are towns."

"And small motels?"

He held his breath while she considered.

She knelt on her seat, the better to lean forward and press her lips softly to his ear, the rasp of his cheek, the indentation of his temple. " 'Amarillo by Morning.' "

That's where they were heading. That's where they'd wake up tomorrow. Cole spared a glance at the road; he studied her sweet face a lot longer. She was giving him more than he deserved. He wanted her to know what it meant to him.

He warned her away with a growl when she splayed her finger on his shirt buttons. "Sit down a minute."

"What's the magic word?" She cocked a brow and made a small moue with her luscious lips.

It was dueling eyebrows. He cocked his higher. She sat.

"I want to say something," he stated.

She arranged her skirt primly over her knees and folded her hands in her lap. "I'm all ears."

She was all woman, and his raking gaze said he knew it.

"I just wanted you to know—" He cleared his throat and twisted his palm around the steering wheel until the plastic squeaked. Where was that cowboy hat when he needed it? He glanced over his shoulder at the backseat. A map draped over the Stetson's bulge.

"You were saying?"

He turned back to the road. This should be easier than staring into her eyes over a candlelit dinner. All the same, he felt her gaze on his profile. "I, uh, meant what I said about wanting you."

She lazily scraped her fingernails up his biceps. His cotton shirt irritated his skin like burlap. He wanted to peel it off right there.

He swallowed again. "More."

"More?"

Her dancing eyes teased him again. He caught her hand in his. "What I meant is, it's more than just wanting you. I wanted you to know that."

Her soft blue eyes held his gaze longer than was prudent. A farm truck honked. Cole swerved.

"I'm not quite sure what you mean," she said.

She was going to make him spell it out. "There are no guarantees," he said.

"I wasn't asking for any."

"Who knows if we'll work this out?"

"We have to start somewhere."

"So why do I feel I passed start a long way back?"

Her optimism never failed. His doubts never stopped. He squinted hard at the road. The wind blew dust devils across the fields.

She leaned over and turned on the radio to the softest country/rock station she could find. "Lot of static."

"Must be a storm between the station and us." He didn't want to talk about radio reception.

Neither did she. She stroked his cheek. "I'm beginning to like your silence."

He gritted his teeth against the emotion her touch generated. "You didn't like it last night."

They'd both hurried to their rooms at opposite ends of the building.

"It hardly compared to the kiss by the Mississippi." She grinned. "Kiss by the Mississippi. That's fun to say." She touched him again. "Even more fun to remember."

How was he supposed to tell her he loved her without getting himself laughed out of the car? His scowl deepened.

Her voice softened. "You're very romantic, you know."

"More than you'll ever know."

"I was hoping I'd find out." Her hand moved to his leg.

"Keep touching me there, and you'll find out before we cross the state line."

She lifted her fingertips from his thigh. "I'm doing it again."

His head jerked right. "What?"

She bit her lip, her hands fists in her lap. "I'm sorry. I go too far."

"I said that wasn't your fault."

"It is. Everyone tells me. I get wrapped up in relationships instead of letting them develop slowly, naturally."

If that was her attitude, she'd never believe he'd fallen in love at first sight. She'd think he'd been desperate, lonely, dying a little before she came into his life. He'd be at a loss to tell her otherwise. He'd taken one look at her and seen life walk in.

"We can go any speed we want," he said.

She turned away, her hair glistening as she looked out the window at the passing plains. "There's no set limit."

"No romance police."

"None. All's fair—"

"Then what are we arguing about?"

"I don't want to make another mistake. Smother you. Baby you. Do everything in this relationship— including assuming it is one."

He peered at the clouds ahead. A thin band gathered on the horizon.

"I should warn you, Cole. I overdo everything when it comes to men."

"You've been holding your own so far."

"I want you to stop me. Tell me when I'm hovering, overcompensating—"

"For what?"

She opened her palms to the gloomy sky. "I don't know. I think I'm contributing, empathizing, thinking ahead, and yet somehow I end up doing all the work. I put too much into my relationships." She sighed. "I didn't think it was possible to love too much."

Cole glowered. "It is."

"See what I mean?"

He didn't see the road anymore, or the clouds growing in the distance. He saw the mountains of Montana, the house he hated coming home to after school, a woman who loved a man so much, she forgave him every outrage.

"What about you?" Evie asked.

He tilted his head.

"What about the women in your life?"

He shrugged. "There've been a few."

"Too few?"

"Nobody I got too close to."

"Was that their doing or yours?"

"You're persistent."

"Journalism degree. Who, what, where, when." She tilted her nose in the air when he slanted her a look. "Just curious."

A woman's "just curious" was worse than a cop's "confess." At least the cops used to read him his rights before rousting him from whatever alley he'd slept in. Evie lured him out of his emotional refuge, tugging him toward the light. "Only one woman lasted more than a few weeks."

"You must wear them out."

A sly grin. "Very funny."

"Why did the one last longer?"

He'd never really put it in words. He wasn't proud of the ones he came up with. "Because she let me keep my distance. She didn't want much."

Evie looked at the sky ahead without seeing it. She listened closely, her body as still as the air outside. She used a method she applied to product testing—check out prior complaints. "So why did you need distance?"

The first raindrops splatted against the windshield.

"I'd been on the road for three years," he said. "I joined the army at nineteen. When I got out I thought it was time to settle down. I never managed to get married. Kathy and I moved in together. Turns out I wasn't ready for that either."

"Was she upset?"

"Not really. I'd made sure she never got close. Protecting her from me, I guess."

"You're confusing yourself with that creep known as your father."

Grim smile. "True. And you?"

"A few longer relationships. One never really went past dating. I kept hoping. He kept making excuses. The commitment thing."

"A man will commit when he's ready."

"You might be right. Jack married a co-worker six weeks after we broke up. I spent months wondering how they got their invitations printed up so fast. Shows how silly I was. They must have been working up to it all along."

She watched the lines darken on his brow. "I don't want to sound self-pitying, Cole. It would've never worked in the long run. Unfortunately I didn't see that at the time."

Cole uncurled his fingers from the wheel, signaling her to be silent. She drew in a slightly huffy breath. He let out a shaky one.

"What?"

"Stop talking."

"What?"

He'd been thinking of mountains, of the darkness that fell when the sun dipped behind them. That black ridge growing on the horizon was no distant mountain range. This was Oklahoma. Sunsets lingered for hours on the prairie. He hadn't noticed the greenish tint to the light until now. A dirty-brown heaviness hung in the air like smog.

Suddenly a crackle of lightning split the clouds in two. Faster than he could say storm, hail the size of gravel hit the windshield. Evie jumped.

"It's like driving in a tin can," she shouted, reaching in the glove box to make a note.

"Don't."

She looked at him in surprise.

"There's no time."

She followed his straight-ahead gaze. The storm had swallowed them up, buffeting the car with wind and splattering it with angry rain. Cole searched for a place to pull off, something sheltered. Under the wide-open Oklahoma sky, there was nowhere.

That's when Evie saw what Cole had ruthlessly ignored, a twisting, dancing funnel cloud corkscrewing down from the clouds to the north.

"Cole?"

He refused to look at it. "It may not come this way."

She reached for his arm. "Cole."

He hissed a curse under his breath. They pulled off the road. "We can't stay in the car," he shouted.

She nodded. The hail stopped as suddenly as it came on. The car grew eerie and quiet. The only sound was the keening wind.

Black and twisting, the funnel coiled like a giant cobra, an obscene belly dancer gyrating across the land.

It heaved and swelled, kicking up puffs of dust and dirt with its narrow tail, dragging down the bruised purple clouds above it.

"We've got to get to cover," Cole said, his voice oddly calm.

"Where?" The landscape was barren. In the distance, well beyond the tornado's path, a lone silo divided the earth from the sky. There was nothing else.

"If it turns this way, we hit the ditch."

"We're going to wait?"

They didn't wait long. The noise grew, a freight train bearing down, a furious bellowing beast at full roar.

Cole shouldered open his door. He dragged Evie out the far side after him. They bent against the wind, his arm around her waist as they staggered across the road to a ditch.

He shouted something about getting farther from the car. Evie made the mistake of looking back. The tornado was gaining on them. The pale Conquest rocked in the wind.

Eyes shut tight against the stinging dust, she tripped and screamed. The ground fell away. Cole slid her down a steep gully. At its base sat a cement culvert.

She ducked into the man-made tunnel. Cole held her back. "Flash floods," he shouted. A rushing trickle of water already filled the bottom of the ditch, swirling around their ankles.

"What do we do?"

He tugged her to his body, leaning them against the storm side of the gully. "Maybe it'll dance over us."

She looked at him in horror. Dance was hardly the word.

He stared into her wide eyes. The rain had started again, pelting them. In seconds they were soaked. It hardly mattered. Not when he saw the trust in her eyes. For some crazy reason she wasn't afraid.

His heart cracked. All his life he'd told himself he never wanted a woman looking at him that way. He'd run from it two nights earlier on the banks of the Mississippi. He'd run from it when he was sixteen. At that moment he would've thrown everything he had to the howling winds just to hold her there in his arms. He was no hero. How the hell could he tell her he was as helpless as she was?

He didn't. There were no words to shout down a tornado. He pulled her close, kissing her harder than the hard earth, surer than the ground turning to mud beneath their feet. Her breasts flattened against his chest, her legs entwined with his. Heat rocketed through his bloodstream. This was all he needed. All he had to have.

He raked her neck with kisses while the storm clawed the fields. He drank her in the way the parched earth drank the rain. In seconds the hill at her back was slippery shining clay. Cole dug his fingers into the crumbling wall, holding them there, wedging his body into hers. Cleansing rain scoured them. Her dress plastered to her body. His shirt stuck to his chest.

Then her hands were there, unbuttoning it, her palms surprisingly hot where she splayed her fingers through the glistening hair on his chest. He wasn't half as gentle with her. He couldn't have unbuttoned a button if his life depended on it. His hands shook and his body pounded. Which part was desire and which part thundering storm, he couldn't have said. He just knew he had to have her—the storm be damned, the past be damned.

Reverently, brazenly, she sank to her knees. Her mouth slaked his chest, her lips forming around a nipple. His body quaked. Gripping her arms, he hauled her back up. She wasn't doing this alone. He pawed a handful of her skirt, roughly sliding it up her thigh. She placed her hand over his, guiding him up under it to a strip of damp silk, a honeyed moistness. One long slow stroke of his finger and she shook.

It was the last slow thing he did. Later he'd remember a blur of heat, wetness, mud, and desire. She asked him wordlessly, urgently, to make love to her. Not even a tornado could have stopped him.

Evie bowed her head. The shower pulsated, blasting her with warm water. She braced her back against the shockingly cool tiles. Her nipples pebbled almost painfully. She welcomed the sensation. For the first time in a life of travels, she didn't think of mildew or athlete's foot or this small motel's cleanliness standards. She closed her eyes and let the water spurt rhythmically against her skin.

Even that seemed too intimate. Alone in a bathroom quickly filling with steam, she folded her arms across her middle and pressed her legs together. What had she done? In a screeching howling terror of a storm she'd made love to Cole Creek. In the mud and the swirling water, their bodies had come together.

She should have been frightened. She'd seen nothing but Cole. The wind had keened and screeched. Sound had come from every direction and no direction, buffeting them, tearing at them. Water had lapped and rushed by their ankles, rising rapidly.

She'd surged with it. Unleashed, untamable, she'd gone into his embrace. She'd done things she'd never dreamed. Unzipping his jeans, she'd reached for him, feeling him buck in her grasp, glorying at the feel of his mud-slick hands gliding over her hips, cupping her, lifting her. The rain was cold, their flesh hot. In the bellowing storm she never heard her panties tear or felt them disappear. She remembered that one moment when he'd paused, his body throbbing and hot against the inside of her thigh. There was nothing there to block him, no silk, no protection, no second thoughts.

The sound of the shower penetrated her memories. Evie looked down at her hands, the brown line of clay and mud beneath her nails. She didn't even want to think about her hair. Gritting her teeth, she stepped away from the wall and stood square beneath the shower. Bowing her head, she let it blast the grime away.

Shaking her head, she spit out water. What had she been thinking?

Nothing. Everything. She'd let the urgency of the moment take over. She'd clung to him as if he were life itself. She'd given him everything.

She moaned. *She'd done it again.*

Soap stung the corner of her eye as if in reproach.

Again didn't apply. She'd never given a man that much. Despite every lie she'd told herself for the last two years, despite every lecture, she'd never learned her lesson. She didn't *want* to be careful in love. She wanted passion, complete, soul-scouring demanding passion. With their lives hanging in the balance, she'd wanted Cole.

But what did he want? She'd felt his answering passion. She felt it still. Rubbing a smudge off her thigh, she realized it was a faint bruise. Her legs shook when she remembered him inside her. Her body clutched, tiny rills of excitement running through her again and again.

Despite the long silent drive into this little town, the excitement had never entirely abated. The storm had blown over. The devastation inside her remained.

She closed her eyes, turned, and let the water beat down her back. Their passion spent, they'd leaned back against the gully wall for untold minutes. She had no idea how long it had been since the storm passed or how long it had taken for Cole to speak.

"Time to go," he'd said.

She couldn't tell how he felt. Her conscience warned her not to read too much into this. Her well-worn list of relationship how-tos ordered her not to pester him for responses. She ached to find out.

He'd helped her to her feet, tugging her skirt down. He'd looked grim, shamefaced. She didn't wonder why. Grit and mud clung to her thighs with the heavy clamminess of soaked fabric. Above the gully's rim, across the road, the car sat patiently where they'd left it. "Can we credit Detroit with that?" she asked.

"Make a note."

Strained jokes didn't help. With the scent of torn-up earth hovering in the air, the car smelled strange inside, its new-car smell as sweet and familiar as coming home.

Cole drove at a measured pace, putting mile after mile behind them and the ditch. They passed through a small town. Its one block downtown was a disaster of broken glass and missing roofs. A pickup truck had been thrown through the front window of a dry cleaner as if it were a giant toy. Its wheels spun slowly. Above it a crooked sign read NEW DRIVE-THROUGH SERVICE.

Ten miles out of town they found a motel in the middle of nowhere. Cole checked them in. He didn't bother with separate rooms. Unlocking the door, he told her she could use the shower first. She headed straight for the bathroom, unable to think of anything to say.

Standing in the shower, she wondered how long it would take to put her world back together. Towns weren't the only things smashed by the storm. She felt as if she'd been blown apart, her defenses rubble, her jagged foundations exposed to his pitiless unblinking gaze.

She ran a hand through her hair. After a fifteen-minute shower it was so clean it squeaked. She pressed her back against the tile once more. She couldn't stay in there forever.

Cole knocked.

She caught her breath.

"Are you okay in there?"

She clamped her hand over her mouth, stifling a laugh that threatened to become a sob. They'd just made love in the mud and the rain while a tornado raged past them like a giant throwing a temper tantrum. She didn't think she'd ever be okay again.

Lose Yourself In 4 Steamy Romances and *Embrace A World Of Passion — Risk Free!*

Here's An Offer To Get Passionate About:

Treat yourself to 4 new, breath-taking romances free for 15 days. If you enjoy the heart-pounding and sultry tales of true love, keep them and pay only our low introductory price of $1.99*.

That's a savings of $12.00 (85%) off the cover prices.

Then, should you fall in love with Loveswept and want more passion and romance, you can look forward to 4 more Loveswept novels arriving in your mail, about once a month. These dreamy, passionate romance novels are hot off the presses, and from time to time will even include special edition Loveswept titles at no extra charge.

Your No-Risk Guarantee

Your free preview of 4 Loveswept novels does not obligate you in any way. If you decide you don't want the books, simply return them and owe nothing. There's no obligation to purchase, you may cancel at any time.

If you continue receiving Loveswept novels, all future shipments come with a 15-day risk-free preview guarantee. If you decide to keep the books, pay only our low regular price of $2.66 per book*. That's a <u>savings of 24%</u> off the current cover price of $3.50. Again, you are never obligated to buy any books. You may cancel at any time by writing "cancel" across our invoice and returning the shipment at our expense.

Try Before You Buy

Send no money now. Pay just $1.99* after you've had a chance to read and enjoy all four books for 15 days risk-free!

*Plus shipping & handling, sales tax in New York, and GST in Canada.

Save 85% Off The Cover Price on 4 *Loveswept*® Romances

Get 4 Loveswept Romances

For The *Low Introductory Price*

Of Just $**1.99**

*Plus shipping & handling, sales tax in New York, and GST Canada.

Titles yo~~u~~ receive ma~~y~~ differ fro~~m~~ those show~~n~~ here, bu~~t~~ will b~~e~~ the late~~st~~ Loveswe~~pt~~ selections

No Risk. No obligation to purchase. No commitment.

EIGHT

Cole walked back to the bed. He'd sat there the last twenty minutes, head in his hands, wondering what the hell had possessed him. The muddy spot on the bedspread caught his attention. He should have thought to put a towel on it.

There was a lot he hadn't stopped to think about. Protection for one. Common sense for another.

With Evie's body wrapped around his, the storm pawing the ground like a raging bull, he'd thought of nothing but loving her. He'd driven into her, thrusting until the mud slid and undulated beneath their writhing bodies. Pure, primal, primitive, he'd fought the fear of losing her with the fear of never having had her, of never letting her know what he'd felt that first time he saw her. What he felt still. The storm unleashed it, personified it. He couldn't hold back.

He grimaced and paced to the motel-room door. He hoped to hell she hadn't heard him say "I love you." He'd shouted it when the storm seemed headed right at them. He'd groaned it when he thrust inside her. He'd hardly heard himself beneath the wind's infernal howl. Had she? Maybe he'd misread the look in her eye that said she felt the same.

"Or did you dream it?" He raked a hand over his face and scowled in the mirror above the low dresser.

After that kiss in Dodge City he'd been speeding, racing toward the inevitable. The temperature in the car had hovered around a hundred and ten. If they had idiot lights for a man's sex drive, his would've glared red.

He'd held back, just enough willpower to keep his foot on the gas pedal. He'd talked to her, shown her a part of himself that wasn't hormones, explained about past loves, communicated. He'd read that this was what women wanted. He'd wanted her to know he wasn't some Neanderthal hot to get her in bed.

"Face it, you were scared." He strafed the motel room with a glance. This was the prime reason he'd kept them moving. He hadn't wanted to take her to some cheap motel. He'd been thinking Amarillo. Picturing a bridal suite, soft music, a two-person tub. A place a man could tell a woman he'd fallen crazy in love and couldn't explain it but hoped the decor might. A champagne-and-roses kind of place.

Instead he'd given her mud and ooze and a shower stall to wash off in. Was it any wonder she was in no hurry to come out? For all he knew she'd snuck out the window and run for the nearest police car.

The shower stopped. Cole waited. Even before she opened the door, his lungs filled with steam, eddying, dissolving, choking.

Wrapped in a towel she'd twisted into a tight knot above her breasts, with another draped across her shoulders, she tiptoed toward the bed. "Your turn," she said brightly. She didn't look at him.

Sidling down the narrow space between bed and wall, she pulled her suitcase closer. The lid popped up like a raised shield.

Cole indicated the bucket of ice and two Dr Peppers. Not exactly Dom Pérignon. "I brought your bag in," he said unnecessarily.

"Thanks." She pawed through her purse for a comb. "I could use some clean clothes."

Was she saying this was all his fault?

Who else's would it be?

He trod into the bathroom and shut the door. His wet shirt slammed against the far wall with an unsatisfying smack. It dropped limply to the floor, leaving yet another muddy stain in its wake.

Viciously twisting a faucet, Cole hissed a curse under his breath. A man didn't treat the woman he loved that way. He didn't overwhelm her when her guard was down, get her in a situation where she couldn't say no.

A man didn't shrivel up inside when she refused to look him in the eye.

Lying in his arms afterward, she'd said nothing. Sitting on the passenger side of the car in her ruined dress, she'd said less than that for ten whole miles. At present she sat on the bed trembling. It was hitting her —what might have happened, what had. He should have said something, asked how she was.

His talkative Evie wasn't talking. Maybe that was all the answer he needed.

He wrenched the faucet marked HOT to the left and let pure cold punish his skin. Tornadoes. Ha. He was the one who'd blown it. Worse than the circumstances, worse than the dirt and the sad-sack amenities, was the fact he couldn't kid himself. She'd heard him say "I love you." In the bedroom, embarrassed to meet his gaze, she'd silently let him know she wanted none of it.

Evie crossed her ankles when the bathroom door opened. Legs extended on the bed, she balanced her back against the headboard. The lobster pink had faded from her skin. Her legs stuck out beneath her shorts; her man-style shirt covered everything else. She'd been rolling and unrolling the cuffs, turning up the collar, folding it down. She'd unbuttoned and rebuttoned the top two. "He loves me. He loves me not."

He emerged when she had two down and nowhere to go. She fiddled with the collar point, resting her gaze on her knobby knees.

"You okay?"

She wiggled her toes inside ankle socks and tennis shoes. "I lost my sandals."

"I'm sorry."

Oh, she hated that tone. She buried her shaky hand in the crook of her arm and stared at him. She didn't want him apologizing. What they'd had had been incredible. Saying it would sound like a cliché.

He stood before the low dresser with its tilted mirror, shoulders hunched, head bowed, jeans low on his narrow hips. She scanned his bare back, her cheeks flushing when she saw the thin scratches her nails had etched there.

So he'd said he loved her in the heat of passion. At the moment he literally turned his back. Although it would be wonderful to believe everything she heard, Evie wasn't that naive. He might have said what he thought she wanted to hear. He even might have meant it. At the time. It was her response that had chased him away—her all-out, give-everything, don't-look-back hurry to love someone.

To love *him*. Even though her eyes stung and her pride shrank with every silent scolding, she wanted to touch him, to get that slouch out of his shoulders, to let him know she would not under any circumstances hold him to those hasty words.

"They were just sandals."

"About what happened. I didn't mean to—"

"Don't. You don't have to." She closed her shirt collar, her skin clammy. "I am a grown woman. I can face facts. These things happen." And no man wanted to get caught because of an infatuation that got out of hand. "Let me make it easy on you. We're two adults. Things got away from us."

He unzipped the shaving kit from his duffel bag. He found a comb and slicked his wet hair back on both sides.

"I'm not reading anything into it. I promise, Cole."

He dropped the comb. "Then I'm not an opportunistic son-of-a-bitch who took advantage?"

"Hardly."

"You weren't in any position to turn me down."

"I never said I wanted to."

"The storm didn't leave you any place to run." He listened to the silence.

She watched the tension knot between his shoulders. "Is that what you think I wanted?"

"A woman should always have a way out."

"That's funny. I've found men are the ones who usually want that."

He twisted at the waist. "This isn't anything against you, Evie."

She halted him with an upraised hand. "It's as personal as it gets. However, we don't have to drag it over the coals."

"If that's what you want."

She wanted to come right out and ask a question without dreading the answer—or worse, making up answers on his behalf. Did he love her? At the moment she didn't have the nerve to ask.

She swung her legs off the bed and fluffed the pillow at her back. "From what I recall, before that tornado hit, we were discussing where all our previous relationships have gone wrong."

"As I recall, we were on our way to the nearest motel." He gripped his razor, stuck halfway between shaving his stubble and packing the whole thing in. "Correct me if I'm wrong, Evie, but the storm wasn't the problem."

She pulled her shoulders back. "I told you I tend to throw myself into relationships. I just want you to know you don't have to worry about it happening with us."

He dropped the razor in the case. The zipper made an ugly scraping sound. "Fine."

"People can go further than they planned. Nothing has to happen between us that we don't both want—"

Like saying "I love you"? Cole thought. He was right. She wanted none of it.

A knock at the door startled them both. Cole strode across the room and took the chain off. The elderly woman from the front desk stuck her head inside. "Excuse me, Mr. and Mrs. Creek?"

He didn't bother correcting her. "Yeah?"

"I know it'd be asking a lot, but there've been some families wiped out. Thank God they're fine, but their trailers were demolished. Since you said you needed showers and towels, I didn't know if you were planning on staying the night—"

"We're done. Give us ten minutes, and we'll be on our way."

"I'd be very obliged. You got off lucky, compared to some."

Evie wondered. Judging from Cole's hurry to get out of there, they'd lost everything.

They drove to Amarillo in silence. The motel's proprietor had given them a couple of threadbare towels to spread on the damp seats. Evie sat on the passenger side. She usually loved driving when she wanted to think. At the moment she preferred curling up, thinking, watching him stare at the road in the glow of the dashboard. A vein beat slowly in his jaw.

She'd meant it when she'd said she wouldn't hold him to his words. There was just one small problem. She was afraid she'd fallen in love with *him*.

She hadn't planned to fall in love. She'd fought the attraction all the way. He was an extremely good-looking man. She could have resisted that. Unfortunately a deep streak of decency, a spine of pure steel, and an unyielding code of personal honor made him very hard not to love. The dose of sexual dynamite they'd shared hadn't helped.

She sighed. Leaning her head against the headrest, she let her lids drift shut. What if he'd meant it? A smoky wisp of hope curled through her. Maybe he was waiting for her to respond. Maybe she was being too careful—

She should be up-front, honest, brave enough to risk a confrontation. Knowing had to be better than suspecting.

Where had she heard that before? Right before her breakup with Jack. And Bill. Every time she confronted a vacillating man, her worst fears came true. She could be blissful while ignorant. Unfortunately, the truth had this sneaky way of coming out eventually.

Ask him.

She opened her mouth. He turned his head, almost as if he'd been waiting, attuned to every move she made, every breath she took.

The words died in her throat. Not tonight. They'd been through so much. His cowboy hat still sat on the backseat. The tornado's roar still rang in her ears. Her body rippled with the aftershocks of their lovemaking. Her heart, impatient and eager, for once remained wise enough to hold back.

He'd registered them in that small motel under a married name, her hopes whispered.

They'd left at the first opportunity.

Because those families needed the room more than they had.

Envying homeless families because they at least had each other was a sure sign that she was being overly emotional. That didn't ease the pain of his not wanting to spend the night with her. He'd headed down the highway for Amarillo as if the tornado had barely deflected their plans.

Night had fallen when she awoke. The outskirts of a city passed by: car lots, bars, repair shops, Mexican restaurants. Cole had turned on the radio. Evie heard the low tones of a man and woman speaking and realized the Austin the announcer referred to wasn't Austin, Texas, but *Austin in the Evening*, the radio show they'd listened to their first night on the road. The psychic, Fiona, was on again.

Evie reached over and turned it off. Cole glanced up in surprise. She watched the neon lining the road. The last thing she needed was a psychic telling her how to get a man to commit. Cole was fully committed to avoiding relationships of any kind. He'd come right out and told her that much of his past. The warning had been the prelude to their lovemaking. She'd be wise to keep that in mind.

"Holiday Inn?" he asked.

"Any chain will do."

He pointed at a billboard. "There's one for thirty dollars a night."

"That should do it." Separate rooms, of course.

She'd stare at the walls. It would give her time to think. "We may get a late start tomorrow. I'll have to write up the tornado story. Ten Safety Precautions If You're Ever Caught in a Storm."

He offered one. "Look for shelter?"

She'd found it in his arms.

"Beware of flash floods."

Especially when dealing with a flood of emotions.

He looked in the rearview mirror, his gaze sliding to her lap.

She loosened her clenched fists. "Just don't call me too early tomorrow morning. It's not as if there's anywhere we have to be."

Yes, there was. Cole knew it the minute she turned that desolate look toward the scenery. They had to find a quiet, thoroughly private place to talk. If talking didn't work, touching might. That meant a room instead of the car.

He cruised by the first chain motel, hoping Evie's increasingly heavy-lidded eyes wouldn't notice his change of course. Her head jerked up when he pulled into a parking lot and shut the engine off. "Are we there?"

"No vacancy at the bargain place."

She peered through the windshield at the tower rising above them. "This is probably the most expensive place in town."

"I'll check it out. You stay here. You look beat."

"But it's my job—"

"You're doing the tornado article instead. Tonight you sleep on a good mattress."

She waved him on, too tired to argue.

Stepping off the tenth-floor elevator fifteen minutes later, Cole let the bellman unlock the door. He deposited Evie's bags at the foot of her bed. Cole swung his duffel off his shoulder and dropped it beside the door.

She searched through her purse for a tip.

"I've got it," Cole said. He slipped an extra five into the man's hand and murmured something as he escorted him out.

There'd been a time, recently, the last few nights, when Evie would have listened more closely, curious to know how far down the hall Cole's room was. She'd have drifted to sleep imagining him in another bed, another look-alike room. She'd have pictured his chest bare, his hands locked behind his head, his eyes staring at the ceiling the way hers had.

She no longer needed to imagine his body. As for sweet nothings, she'd heard him say something earlier that day beyond her wildest imaginings. If only he'd meant it.

She was too exhausted to think silly romantic thoughts without wanting to cry.

"Are you okay?"

She sniffed and grabbed a tissue from the box on the nightstand. "Long day. Standing in the pouring rain probably wasn't the wisest move."

"Not to mention lying in it."

Her laugh came out rusty. He stood at the foot of the only bed, his hands on his hips. His shirt spread taut across his chest. If she never touched him again, she'd die.

"Evie."

She waved him away with the tissue. "If you want to go, it's okay. Your day was as long as mine."

He drew in a long breath and let it hiss out. "Get your clothes off."

Raising a brow felt like lifting a barbell. "Pardon me?"

He strode to the bedside and yanked down the covers. Tossing her suitcase on a chair, he popped it open. "You got a nightie in here?"

Pieces of silk and cotton drifted everywhere as he searched. Panties. Nylons. Evie knew she should be miffed. Perturbed. Some word like that. Her language skills seemed to have shut down along with her sense of dignified outrage.

"Here." He shoved a wrinkled piece of chiffon her way. "Put this on."

Had she really packed that? The baby-doll night-gown dangled from his finger. "I only wear this stuff when I'm traveling."

He grunted.

"At home I don't wear anything."

Something about his glower got her back up. Why should she pretend he hadn't seen a lot more than this nightgown would ever reveal? Or that they hadn't made love under the most extraordinary circumstances? Pretending nothing had happened was not a choice. They had three more weeks in that car.

She unzipped her shorts. Dropping them to her ankles, she kicked them across the room. She unbuttoned the third button on her shirt, then the fourth. Turning her back to him, she pulled it over her head. The nightie wafted down her upraised arms. All he got was a view of her pantie-clad backside.

Then she caught him watching the side view in the mirror.

She pulled the sheets down with a snap. Stuffing her feet under the covers, she pulled a blanket to her chin and clamped it beneath her armpits.

He dropped something on the nightstand.

"I won't need the remote. I'm going straight to sleep."

"Fine."

The car keys landed next to the ashtray.

"You can turn off the light on your way out."

"In a minute." He emptied his pockets. A clatter of spare change landed on the table, right next to his watch.

"What are you doing?"

"Getting ready for bed."

Her mouth fell open. "Don't tell me this is the only room they've got."

"It is."

"Is there a rodeo in town? A convention?"

"I don't know. It's the only room I asked for."

Her heart thumped. He'd caught her up shorter than a roped steer.

He peeled off his shirt. Lowering his jeans, he tossed them over the back of the chair. Naked and totally at ease, he crossed to the bathroom and flicked off the final light.

Evie listened to the rattle of the chain on the door. Footfalls whispered along the carpet. The curtains pulled back, metal rings scraping. Light from the city glowed through the room. "Quite a view," he said.

She stared at his silhouette. He seemed larger in the dark, almost menacing. "I can't sleep with a lot of light."

He closed the curtains.

That was worse. The darkness intensified every sound. She listened past the buzzing in her ears. Shallow breaths rasped in and out. She wasn't sure whose. "I changed my mind. Open the curtains."

His footfalls stopped inches from the bed.

"Please?" She waited.

The curtains scraped open again. "Better?"

"For now."

The mattress sagged as he got in. They both lay still.

"Evie."

"Please, Cole."

"Please what?"

She shut her eyes tight. If they were really lovers, he wouldn't have that wary tone. "I don't want to analyze this. Not now. I overanalyze everything. What men say. What they don't. This isn't the time or place."

He huffed. "If this isn't the place—"

"Please." In the long pause that followed, she heard the soft ticking of her travel alarm.

"Do you want me to leave?"

"No." It came out before she could stop it. There was no point denying it.

The blackness enveloped them like a womb, two voices floating in the dark.

"You don't hate me for today?" he asked.

"You didn't make the tornado."

"We made love. In the mud, the rain."

"Did you hear me complaining?"

"It was hard to hear anything." He waited.

Should she tell him what she *had* heard?

His hand skimmed the back of hers, his fingers twining with hers. The back of his other hand touched her thigh. After a few seconds, he unlaced their fingers and traced the fine hairs up her arm. He turned on his side, found her collarbone with his fingertips, then the sensitive side of her neck. He cupped the swell of her breast beneath the chiffon.

"We don't have to talk about it tonight," he murmured.

A sweet, sad emotion corkscrewed through her. She was about to make a huge mistake, loving a man she hadn't had the courage to talk to. She was giving herself to someone who might or might not love her back, going into this with more hope than guarantees, gullible as ever, more vulnerable than she'd ever felt in her life.

She reached for him, her hand small and cool on his biceps. She squeezed it, silently marveling at the strength. Hard with tension, the muscle twitched. "Are you showing off?"

Cole heard the grin in her voice and something eased inside him. He shifted closer, his leg alongside hers, his mouth brushing her lips. "I'm sorry today wasn't better."

Her laugh came from someplace deep in her throat. "It's never been better. Ever."

NINE

She dreamed they were driving, the road humming, the car vibrating. The thoroughly sexy feel of power at her fingertips seduced her. Her hand closed around the slick polished knob of the gearshift. Wind whistled through the window. Her hair blew across her forehead. Her skin was flushed, hot, her chest heavy. . . .

Her eyes opened. Cole whistled a soft breeze across her cheek before kissing it. "Morning."

She groaned. He was already dressed, the sun long up. She hadn't even brushed her teeth. She threw an arm over her face. "Go away."

"You didn't say that last night."

He didn't need to remind her. Not another word about love had been mentioned. They'd done everything else. "Are you going to blackmail me?"

He chuckled a satisfied male chuckle. As he walked across the room she would've gladly tossed a pillow at his cocky head. She suddenly felt too snug, and too smug, to move. They'd made tender love through the night. Soft, slow, satiny love that had built like a slow pulse. He'd kissed her intimately, showing her all the ways he hadn't been able to love her in the storm's fury.

She smiled sleepily at the memory. She'd never imagined him being gentle. But tenderness with Cole still harbored an undercurrent of urgency, of reined-in passion. She shuddered deep inside, remembering the culmination of that exquisitely prolonged embrace. Curling on her side, she inhaled his deliciously spicy scent on the pillow.

"Scoot. Breakfast."

She propped open an eye. A blurry breakfast tray swam into view. The scent of bacon and eggs filled her nostrils. The sight of Cole's chest, peppered with crinkly gold hair, made her mouth water. Shifting onto her stomach, she wedged herself up on her elbows. "Food? At this hour?"

"Muffins. Juice. Toast. Eggs. Whatever turns you on."

Cole Creek, the top button of his jeans undone, topped her list. She swiped a falling lock of hair out of her eyes. "Get me a robe, please."

"There's one in the bathroom. I'll get it."

She sat up properly, her knees under the tray, her mouth curved in a shy smile at the one item he hadn't mentioned, a red rose in a narrow vase.

He tossed her the terrycloth robe and sat at the foot of the bed. He clicked on the TV, channel-surfing for a weather report. "Which way today, kemo sabe?"

"Go west, young man."

"New Mexico?"

"Then Arizona. I want to see the Grand Canyon."

"It'll be dark by the time we get there. I don't think they floodlight it."

"We'll do it in two days. Besides . . ." She wiped a drop of butter from the corner of her lip, flushing pink at the way he licked his own lips in response. "Besides, I need to spend this morning typing up the tornado article. If the magazine plays their cards right, they might put it out on the wire services. Get some publicity for when the monthly issue comes out."

Cole took the hint, handing her her laptop. "You know what they say about all work and no play."

"I am not dull."

"Not with me you're not."

He reached across the bed. It was his turn to wipe a smear of jam off her lower lip. Her tongue darted nervously to catch the cloying sweetness. It contacted with the callused pad of his index finger. She put off her writing for another hour and they let the food get cold.

She emerged from the shower to find him changing out of gray shorts in the middle of the room. "How was the gym?"

"Super. I never lifted so much weight."

"The wonders of testosterone."

He flexed a biceps, resting his forehead on his fist. "Look good?"

"Lovely, Arnold. I'll make a note."

"How'd the article go?"

"Fast."

"Like us?"

She shivered as he came up behind her, his hands resting on her shoulders. He drew her robe open, nibbling as he went. "Hope I didn't rush you."

"I kind of liked it," she murmured, aghast at the breathlessness he produced in her. Whose fault was it if she melted at the slightest graze of his lips?

She reached up, tousling his hair with her fingertips. In seconds she dug her fingers deeper, luxuriating in the love bites he tracked down her neck. Tingles broke out all over her skin, shivering across her breasts, racing down her abdomen to a patch of heat on her thighs. She traced the sensation inch by dizzying inch.

She dimly realized he'd paused, his hands clenched tight on her upper arms. "What is it?" she asked.

He said nothing.

The sizzling sensations cooled. "Cole?"

"Did I do this?"

The ugly rasp in his voice made her turn. He dropped the embrace, glowering at her collarbone. She wrapped the robe across her breasts, then gingerly turned to the full-length mirror on the wall. A row of small bruises dotted the ridge of her shoulders. She covered them with her hand, as if hiding them would make him forget.

"I hurt you."

"I think it happened during the storm. We got a little carried away."

"What do you mean *we*?"

"You didn't hurt me, Cole."

He tugged her hand away, twirling her to the mirror. "You're black-and-blue."

"They're love bites."

He pulled the robe to her waist, the violence directed more at himself than her. "And this one? What about the one on your arm? How many other places, Evie?"

She knew a beauty of a bruise graced her thigh, but that was due to a rock the storm had exposed on the gully slope. Cole had never meant to press her into it; he hadn't even known it was there.

The bruises were. "It's not as if you did it deliberately."

His stare could have turned lava to cold stone. "Where have I heard that before?"

"Cole."

He strode across the room, packing his duffel with fistfuls of clothes. "No woman should put up with being hurt in the name of love."

"I know that. But there is a difference between love play and deliberately hitting someone."

" 'It wasn't his fault,' " he repeated caustically. " 'That's just the way it is.' 'His emotions get the better of him.' 'He can't help it.' "

"Stop it."

He strangled the duffel by yanking on the drawstring. "We have to get going."

"We aren't going anywhere until we settle this."

"Then we'll be stuck in Amarillo for a long time, Evie. This goes back a lot further than a few days."

Funny what hurt and what didn't. Driving toward the western border of Texas and into northern New Mexico, Evie flinched at his reference to their relationship as "a few days." As far as she was concerned they'd made memories she'd carry with her long after a handful of bruises had faded.

That struck her as funny, too, in a dismal sort of way. She'd spotted the bruises in the mirror after her shower. The sensual memories they evoked had made her quiver. To her they were symbols of uninhibited release, a passion she'd never experienced. To Cole they were black marks from the past.

The argument reignited as soon as they crossed the border.

"I bruise easily," she explained in her most rational tone.

"Don't blame yourself!"

His shout quelled her momentarily. The spurt of anger that raced to her defense surprised her even more. "Cole, people look at me hard and I bruise. Half the time I don't even know what I bumped into."

"Me this time."

"And never again. Is that what you're saying?"

"Don't tell me you like pain."

She'd never heard a man more contemptuous. He directed every ounce of venom at himself. Apparently there was no correct thing to say. "They're called love bites."

"Call it love and anything's allowable, is that it?"

"As I recall, you mentioned something about love at the time."

He speared her with a glance. "Real love never hurts."

"A wonderful sentiment but hardly true."

"Tell me about it. It was my mother's motto. She

claimed it wasn't Dad beating her up, it was another part of him. As if he could be excused for what his fists did."

"You're not him. Do you think I'd put up with it for a minute if you were?"

"You're handing me plenty of excuses."

"I know how to draw the line."

"Except where love is concerned."

That stung. For all the wrong reasons. She did tend to make excuses for men: why they didn't call, why they missed dates, why they wouldn't make commitments. Was she doing the same for him? "I'd never put up with violence."

"You already have. You're black-and-blue, Evie!"

Incensed, she unbuttoned her blouse with one hand, steering with the other. Yanking the blouse off her right shoulder, she scooted forward to see her collarbone in the rearview mirror. "Look at these! Are these fist marks? They're hickeys for heaven's sake!"

A horn honked. She nearly drove off the road. With the mirror tilted down, she'd never seen the truck come up behind them. She whipped her head around. The trucker cruised up alongside. He mimed a strip-tease, leeringly suggesting she bare the other shoulder next.

Cole leaned across her lap and gave the man a succinct hand gesture. The trucker mouthed a few choice words and passed them in a clatter of tiny stones.

Evie resumed her driving, hauling her blouse up her arm. "Jerk," she muttered under her breath.

"That's about it."

"I wasn't talking about you."

"You don't have to."

She could tell from his scowl that he'd been calling himself every name in the book since Amarillo. "I am not letting you blame yourself for something we were both involved in."

"Great. *You* take responsibility for *my* actions. That way I can keep right on doing it."

"Are you paranoid about this or what? You are not your father. By now you should have figured that out. Tell me, have you ever hit a woman?"

His pause made a queer chill run down her spine.

"Well?" She wasn't caving in this time. They'd shared too much for her to hide behind politeness. "I have a right to know."

"I've hit men."

"When?"

"A couple of guys who picked me up hitchhiking. A drunk in a truck stop." He paused. "I hit my old man once."

"Never a woman."

"Never."

"Then why does this unhinge you?"

"It doesn't. You do."

Evie waited until dinner to follow up on his remark. There were too many issues bubbling over to sort out why that one phrase haunted her. Was it possible she got to him the way he'd gotten to her? She was so afraid to show her feelings lest they run over as they always had in the past. Worse, she didn't want to begin reading into his expressions, creating feelings where none existed.

In the calm that settled over the Albuquerque restaurant overlooking the Rio Grande, she stuck to a travelogue recap of the day's drive. "I never realized how beautiful the desert could be. Still, I don't see how people can live without trees. Do cactus count as trees?"

"Huh?"

"You're a sparkling dinner companion."

He rubbed a hand over his face. "I heard you. The desert's fine if you're in an air-conditioned car with a full tank of gas."

"You hitched across it?"

"In the dead center of summer. Not a wise idea."

She hefted a carafe. "More water?"

He grinned. "You read my mind."

"It was the image of those parched lips. The circling buzzards. The bleached bones."

"Very funny. I was a kid from Montana, a mountain goat. What did I know about deserts?" He drained a beer and eyed her thoughtfully. "I kept expecting to come across an oasis."

"And did you?"

He looked at her as if she were one, a cool pool of water to slake a man's thirst after a lifetime of looking.

She finger-combed her hair from her eyes; whispery whiffs floated down again. "Tell me about it."

"Running away?"

"Life on the road."

"It's a different world. Walking. Being on your own. All that sky. All that asphalt and concrete." He shrugged. "I came out the other side of it alive. That was all that mattered at the time. It got to the point at home where I was going to have to leave or—"

"Or what?"

"Or kill my old man."

"So you left."

"Forever." He planted his elbows on the table, hunching his shoulders over his empty plate. "Even after he was dead, my mother didn't want me back. I guess she preferred her memories of him." He shook his head. "Her funeral was three years ago. I didn't even go back for that."

Evie touched his hand without thinking. He let her. A long moment passed. "Do you want to?"

"What?"

"Drive through Montana."

He considered it. Wadding up a napkin, he tossed it toward the ashtray. "No. Better let sleeping dogs lie."

"Nothing to hurt you there now."

"Just memories."

She traced the shiny soup spoon beside her plate, musing at how it distorted her reflection. "Are the memories there or do you carry them wherever you go?"

"Touché, Mrs. Freud."

She knit her brows and tried an appropriately Germanic accent. "Ze memories, zey are not in Mon-ton-ah. Zey are here, no?" She tapped her forehead.

His smile faded. "They're here." He drew a finger along his neck, trailing it over his collarbone—her map of tiny bruises.

"You wouldn't hurt me, Cole."

"No? I could hurt you by saying the wrong thing. By being the wrong man. By letting this go any further."

She paled.

The waitress appeared. "Anything else?"

"Just the check," he said.

Evie wasn't backing down. "If you're doing anything to hurt me, Cole, I will tell you."

She was already letting him off too easy, giving him excuses he couldn't stomach. "We better get a move on. You want to be in Gallup by nightfall."

"Oh yes. Don't want to miss the sunset."

He thought of how cold the desert got at night—and how lonely. Much as he knew he should put some space between them, he took her arm and escorted her from the restaurant, anything to smell her perfume one more time.

It was the simplest question. *How do you feel about me?* Evie couldn't chase it from her mind. They drove toward the orange-and-indigo bands of a dazzling New Mexico sunset, toward a night in another motel. A languid warmth curled through her. She knew they'd share another bed; he'd come to her again. What would it be like this time? How much of herself could she give without telling him the truth? She loved him. Except for that one time, he'd never spoken of love again. How many times had she promised herself she wouldn't cave in to her fear again?

She hoped he'd mistake the silence for awe at nature's beauty. She reached for the radio, scanning the dial for a certain psychic. Nothing.

Fiona stood over the sizzling concoction of sautéed zucchini and soy paste. Since when had healthy become a synonym for unappetizing? She wondered how one added color to this dish without adding calories. "Adding flavor would be nice."

She sighed. Channeling legendary queens and courtesans was one thing. Why couldn't she channel a French chef when she needed one?

Suddenly the white mash congealed into something vaguely resembling mountains. The zucchini piled to the left like a range of evergreens. The soy paste dotted the nonstick surface like snow. She thought of the Rockies and didn't know why.

"Uh-oh." It was never a good sign for love when the mountain symbol came up. It meant daunting, perhaps insurmountable challenges.

One thing she did know was to trust her train of thought. She cleared her mind and waited. Memories of her appearance on Austin in the Evening *floated through. It had been a disappointing return engagement. The mysterious Eve hadn't called.*

Why think of Eve just then? Fiona tilted the frying pan, reading the contents like tea leaves. Interesting. She'd known all along that the man Eve was looking for was right beside her. That didn't seem to have changed. The stormy sensation had dissipated. Now another form of upheaval loomed on the horizon. Bigger than mountains. Rockier than Pike's Peak.

Her nose twitched. She'd burned the zucchini beyond

recognition. She dumped it in the garbage can and popped a vegetarian pizza in the microwave. This psychic business could be frustrating.

"It's a challenge."

"Uh-huh."

Evie curled her fingers around the steering wheel and revved the engine. "Daunting but not insurmountable."

"Whatever you say."

"You think I can't do it?"

He squinted at the hairpin mountain road that awaited them, a ribbon unguarded by a rail, falling off precipitously as it climbed higher and higher through the Colorado Rockies. Evie had insisted on taking a lesser-known route north. She wanted to see what the car could do. "The whole car commercial," she exclaimed. "Deserts, mountains, snow."

From the safety of the foothills it looked as if plenty of early-season snow awaited them.

"You want to take this at sixty," he repeated.

"As long as there's no traffic coming and the pavement's reasonably dry."

"Have you ever heard the phrase *don't try this at home*?"

"My point exactly. We don't have mountains like this in Michigan. However, we do have all-season super-tread tires on this puppy."

"And you have how much driving experience?"

"I took that defensive driving course in Dearborn

three years ago. I was doing a safety feature for the magazine."

"Mm."

"Your faith in me is underwhelming."

He took a deep breath, checked his seat-belt catch, and gestured toward the towering peaks. "Whelm away."

The ride went better than expected. Except for a few tense turns when he longed to reach for the overhead strap, she handled the car with ease—not to mention glee.

"Whew! This is fun."

Another hairpin waited around the next bend—his stomach was sure of it. He rubbed his forehead as if spikes pierced into his brain.

"It's not that bad," Evie said.

"Did I say it was?"

"You look like a dog being tortured by dog whistles."

"It's not far off."

Her driving wasn't the problem. She pushed the eject button and the tape spat out. " 'Rockie Mountain High' is a perfect choice for this leg of the trip."

"If you want to torture your mechanic into submission, it's delightful."

She muttered something about taste. "We could try 'Stairway to Heaven.' "

"How about George Strait?" He switched on an ubiquitous country tune. "Let's not fight about music. Just play something I like."

She laughed. "Does this feel like fighting?"

Actually, it felt good. A little bickering. A few yelps

when she took a corner too fast. None of it dampened her fun. She laughed, gave it some gas, and went into the next turn with total self-assurance. She laughed off his muttered warnings the same way.

It was what Evie had always been, unafraid, willing to face down the world. Nothing like his mother. Any sign of a disagreement would have sent her running, backpedaling, apologizing. Try to corral Evie, and she wouldn't hesitate to tell him where to get off.

"We should stop at the next town," he warned. "This climbing eats into the mileage."

"Let's stop at the pass. There's supposed to be a gorge there."

They'd seen the biggest gorge of all the day before. It was a little disorienting to think that the day before they'd been in the Arizona desert, staring down into the Grand Canyon. Now the air was thin and cold, the pavement glistening with melted snow instead of heat waves, the tires spitting up mist behind them instead of dust. His life seemed to have changed as rapidly and radically as the scenery. For the last two nights they'd slept as one. Their bodies stiff after a day in the car, they'd unwound in each other's arms.

Her bruises faded a bit every day. He wanted to say the same for his.

She glanced over from the steering wheel. "What are you thinking?"

He winced.

"Dreaded relationship question. I know. But you got awful quiet there."

"Just watching the view. It's moving by pretty fast."

"Very funny. I wanted to see how she handles."

He pictured how *she* handled and felt a surge of warmth he'd become accustomed to in the last few days.

"Talk to me."

Another familiar emotion tweaked his conscience. He'd seen the caution in her eyes when she checked the rearview mirror then skidded a glance his way. He sensed the way she drew her shoulders back and dared him to open up to her. It wasn't easy for her, confronting men about their feelings.

"What do you want to know?"

"What we were arguing about a few days ago."

"My parents? I wanted to think I'd left that behind me in Montana. Guess not."

"But you know you're not your father."

"I know." The very idea of having hurt her, even unintentionally, made him sick. "I overreacted. I'd never hurt you, Evie. I want you to know that."

"I do. But—"

The car grew chilly as they passed through the shaded side of a mountain. "But what?"

"You hurt me when you beat yourself up like that. When you won't talk."

"I'm sorry."

"It's okay." She grimaced at his automatic scowl. "I mean, I understand. But it also bothers me—no, ticks me off royally when you act as if I don't have the self-respect to leave a man who'd hurt me. You need to have a little more faith in my taste."

She was one hundred percent right. It wasn't just his father who'd given him a bad impression of marriage. It was his mother's acquiescence in the whole thing.

"Faith in your taste, huh?"

"Mm-hmm." She gave him a coquettish grin, raking his body from bent knees to chest. "I'd say I've got pretty good taste."

TEN

They cruised into a tiny mountain town. A diner with a line of gas pumps outside greeted them. "Fill up outside then fill up inside?" Evie suggested.

"Let me pump it this time. It's my job, remember?"

"I'll get us a booth." Slinging her purse over her shoulder, grabbing the nylon winter jacket she'd brought for the mountains, she waltzed inside and didn't look back.

The restaurant opened into a beamed room the size of a small barn. Checked tablecloths greeted her. Candles in Chianti bottles flickered. The place had a cozy sawdust smell and a roaring fire under a copper hood. Evie wished Cole was there to see it. On the other hand, it gave her a few moments to think about what he'd said.

It's my job. Was that what was bothering him? He'd been dropping comments about his work since the previous day—pointing out the differences between a woman with a college degree and a man with a trade.

What he didn't know was that Bud had been doing some sales talk of his own.

"A little dim in here, isn't it?"

She scooted over and let him slide in next to her in the booth. "There's supposed to be a band. Good sight lines from here."

"I thought you wanted to talk."

She did. She decided to plunge right in. "Guess who I talked to last night?"

He cocked a brow. "Besides me?"

"While you were in the shower."

He shrugged, signaled the waitress for a beer, and comfortably, automatically slid an arm around Evie's shoulders. "Don't tell me you've got a husband back in Michigan."

"Better."

"Better?"

"I've got Bud."

"Bud's a friend," Cole explained.

The waitress grinned and set down a beer and two menus.

"He's also a font of wisdom and information," Evie said when they were alone.

"You've been pumping him."

"Like an oil well. He says you're the best mechanic he's seen, that the computerized gizmos on new cars don't faze you in the least, and that he'd like to leave you the garage when he retires."

"Which will be sometime late in the next century. He's going to die with a wrench in his hand and dirt under his nails, take my word for it."

"It takes one to know one. He says you're the only

man he knows who's more dedicated than he is. Besides, they're retiring to Florida in three years."

"According to Vivian, he's been saying that for ten."

"He says you're smart as a whip, you have the entrepreneurial instincts of Donald Trump, and you've brought in a whole new line of customers."

"Moving into luxury foreign cars is a specialty that'll pay off in the long run. As for the computer stuff—"

Laughing, she set her hand on his arm. "Can I ever get you to say something positive about yourself?"

"I'm explaining—"

"That you're not as wonderful as everyone thinks you are."

"Everyone meaning Bud."

"And me." She let that comment hang in the air. Her heart hung in the balance with it. He wasn't looking at her. Dammit, she *wanted* to go too far this time. She wanted to say what she felt.

"I'm self-educated, Evie."

That much she'd heard.

"I spent four years in the army, four more picking up mechanic jobs. I don't know anything I can't take with me to another place, another job. This is the longest I've stayed in one place."

"Why?"

"Tired of moving on. Tired of looking back."

Evie listened. He'd had a fascinating life. Adventures, resourcefulness, skimping, and making do. Surviving. He'd come out of it sane and levelheaded, a

survivor with rock-hard values his father hadn't destroyed but only strengthened.

And yet—she had this sense that what she was hearing wasn't all he was telling her. There was this sneaky
subtext to every anecdote: he wasn't her type; they
didn't have anything in common. Her family was great,
his screwy. Hers gentle and sensible, his violent and
obsessive. Liking was great but Love was dangerous—
according to Cole.

Evie reminded herself of her tendency to hear what
she wanted to hear. All the same, she felt compelled to
tactfully debate his harsher judgments, substituting
more positive interpretations, speaking up for love.
"Women do not have to be obsessive, all-consuming,
or self-negating. That's not what true love is."

"You could go on a radio show with jargon like
that."

She very nearly had. It amazed her that it had been
a week since she'd first met him. Since she'd turned to
a radio psychic for advice. She'd barely known Cole
then. She learned more all the time. "What your parents had sounds like codependency. Real love is life
affirming, joyous."

Cole suspected as much. He just had a hard time
believing it. Setting down the beer, he glanced at the
menu's burger section. He'd hedged his bets all his life,
holding on to the few things he could pack and carry,
keeping his feelings to himself. Maybe it was time he
dredged up some of Evie's courage. Looking after himself was one thing; risking someone else's feelings another.

He gripped her hand without looking her in the

eye. The waitress came and went. He waited until they were alone again.

"I'm going to need that hand," she joked.

He took the plunge. "If we survive your driving through the mountains—and that's a big if—"

"Ha."

"If we do, I—I've never asked a woman this. I don't know how to put it."

Aware they'd gone beyond just making conversation, she licked her lips and took a fast sip of water. "Yes?"

He'd have to say it fast if he was going to get it out at all. "I want to go to Montana."

She drew in a shaky breath. "Montana?"

"I want you to come with me, to see where I grew up."

It sounded lame. He wasn't saying it right. She'd expected more. He knew it. Maybe they'd get to that altar someday. There were some ghosts he had to lay to rest first.

He squinted her way, expecting disappointment, resignation. Her smile could've lit up the corner of the cavernous room. "I'd love to."

"You mean it?"

She knew exactly what he meant—what it meant to him to share his fears with her. She trailed a finger along his jaw, love shining in her eyes. "I mean it."

He kissed her, not caring who saw or whether their just-delivered dinners got cold. "You're really something, you know that?"

She ducked his next kiss and snapped a napkin open on her lap. "Pass the ketchup, please."

"Evie."

"What?"

"You're going to get coy on me now?"

A superior sniff. Were those tears glistening in her eyes or mountain air? "I don't know what you mean."

"We've said it just about every way we can."

"Said what?"

"What we say at night. I love you. I know—I know you love me." Her head whipped around. "I've seen the look in your eye," he said, "when I'm inside you, when you're twined around me. You love me too."

She flushed three shades of red and tore a piece of breading from her fish. She was a nibbler, and he could make her very nervous. "What do you want me to say?"

"That you love me too."

"I've said that."

"In the heat of passion."

"I've told you, you don't want to hear it. I go overboard."

"And you don't want to with me, is that it?" He washed the bitter taste away with beer.

"I didn't say that. In my experience *I love you*, like *we have to talk*, is a phrase that's guaranteed to send a man running."

"And I'm the original runaway."

She clutched his hand as he reached for the fries. "I've never known a man less likely to run. I trust you, Cole."

"You've known me a week."

She shrugged. "Go figure. I do, though."

"And love?"

"I'm the one I don't trust. I don't want to smother you."

He grinned. Popping a fry in his mouth, he stretched both arms along the back of the booth. "If you're wearing me out, I'll let you know, sugar."

She scolded him with a smile that had a touch too much pride in it. "You said it yourself. You don't want me putting you on a pedestal. That 'my hero' stuff."

He should've known he'd have to pay for that remark. "I stopped worrying about that days ago."

"What do you mean? And wipe that smirk off your face."

It grew. He played his fingers through her hair, watching her shoulder rise as he scraped his thumb down the sensitive side of her neck. "I mean after the grief you've given me the last few days, I think I can trust you to put me in my place."

"That's good?"

He shrugged. "Sixteen years and I never saw my mother do it once. You're not shy about telling me where to get off."

"I told you I wouldn't let you walk all over me."

"I believe you."

Her gaze held his, a sweet smile glimmering in her eyes. "You do?"

"Somewhere between the semi you insisted on passing on the Continental Divide and the curves you've been careening through all morning, I decided you wouldn't back down for anyone."

"That's just the car."

"It's the woman behind the wheel."

She laughed out loud. "Who's on a pedestal now?"

"Some people belong there." He just couldn't tell her how long she'd been on it. He leaned closer, whispering in her ear. "Don't worry. You can come down at night."

She brushed her lips over his. "I plan to."

They sat through the band's first set, in no hurry to get back on the road. Evie mused about overnight accommodations in such a small town.

"We could kill the whole afternoon here," he murmured. "Who says we have to move on?"

"The magazine is going to wonder if I stop submitting receipts for two rooms."

"We only need one."

"But what do I do when they reimburse me for two?"

"Give it to charity. There're some families in Oklahoma who could use it."

"There's an idea."

"Speaking of a waste of money." He pulled a pack of cigarettes from his pocket.

Evie gasped.

"Old habit. I indulge every now and then."

"Why start now?"

"Did you see some of the guardrails we swiped today?" He held his hand out, imitating a nervous tremor. "I need these things for my nerves, honey."

"Don't blame your lung cancer on me. And no smoking in the car."

He rakishly set the cigarette between his lips. "A rare vice. Picked it up in the army."

"Any other bad habits you want to tell me about?"

"Just lovin' you." He grinned and scratched a flame

from a match with his thumb. Inhaling the first drag, he was careful to blow the smoke out of her direction.

"Filthy habit," she said with a sniff.

"Chalk it up to incredible willpower."

"Willpower? Quitting takes willpower."

"Postponing takes more. I've been wanting a smoke since our first time."

"The postcoital nicotine fix?"

"It's tough lighting a match in a tornado."

"And I thought we'd struck enough sparks ourselves."

"Oh, we did, babe. We did."

Evie shook her head and laughed, her voice mellowing to an intimate purr. "How did this become so easy?"

He'd been thinking the same thing. Bantering, bickering, teasing—it was as if a dam had broken. They were suddenly lovers, the shadowboxing first steps behind them. He leaned over to kiss her again. This time she turned her cheek. "Not with smoke on your breath."

"Cut off so soon?"

"If it's not a habit, then giving it up should be easy."

"Changing me already." He crumpled the pack. "Satisfied?"

She crooked a brow at the glowing tip of the one between his fingers. "And that coffin nail?"

"Last one."

"I'll believe it when I see it. Craven addicts can never be trusted."

But women who weren't afraid to speak their minds

could be. Cole would even give up his annual New Year's Eve Havana cigar if it meant having this woman in his life. His hand draped around her shoulder, he let the cigarette dangle off the end of the booth. The band played another song. Evie snuggled into the crook of his arm. He closed his eyes and listened to the one about a man loving a woman. He inhaled the sweet shampoo smell of her hair, the pine scent of the log fire, the acrid smell of nylon melting—

Evie screamed. She whooshed her coat out of the booth and tossed it on the floor. A cowboy from the next table jumped up and stomped on it.

Cole stamped on it for good measure. Sparks scattered across the floor. He waved off the owner, poised to douse the fire with a shiny red extinguisher.

"You set my coat on fire!" Evie wailed.

"I didn't mean to."

"Put that thing out," she commanded.

He rammed his last cigarette in the ashtray.

"And pour water on it."

He doused it with her water glass.

"And stir the ashes."

He paused in midgesture. "What do I look like, Smokey the Bear?"

"You can't be too careful."

"Obviously I wasn't careful enough."

"Okay, folks, show's over," the owner said. He shouldered up beside Cole. "You plan on setting anything else on fire?"

Cole glared.

Evie stared at her charred coat, a hand clamped to

her mouth. Her gaze slid to the floating ashtray then Cole.

"Go ahead. Read me the riot act."

Her hand couldn't stifle a bubble of laughter. She replaced it with a stern frown. "I can't believe you just did that."

"I don't mind setting you on fire," he muttered, "I never meant your wardrobe any harm."

She gingerly picked up his victim by the zipper.

"Is it a total loss?"

"Not if I need a vest." The blackened stump of a sleeve flopped to the floor, the down stuffing protruding. "I've heard of passion igniting but not nylon!"

"I'll buy you another."

"It was a London Fog. Guess it's a London Smog now." She laughed and shook her head, assessing his hangdog look. "It was an honest mistake, Cole."

"More like a major bonehead blunder. Let's get out of here."

He looked so contrite, she let him pick up the check.

"No staying overnight?"

"Not in this state. Let's see if we can make the border by sundown."

She was still laughing when they drove out of town. "Look at this! An inch of snow since we stopped for lunch!"

"You can get that in the mountains. It must've fallen while we were inside."

"And it was so toasty by the fire," she mused.

"Don't start."

She chuckled, not the least cowed by his thundering scowl. "Cole, it's not as if you did it on purpose."

"Could we not talk about it?"

Evie grinned, more to herself than him.

A dozen twisting miles outside town he turned the heater up. "You're going to freeze without a coat."

"I'll just think of you and all the sparks you ignite."

"Very funny."

She chuckled, suddenly blissfully happy. "I thought so."

"You want my coat?"

"I'll manage. I assume there's not a lot of shopping in Yellowstone."

"Bozeman, Montana, is the next big town."

"I'll survive."

"How's this?" He reached for a nob and nodded toward her lap. "Feel warmer?"

Automatically. All he had to do was rake her with his gaze. She gradually realized another warm sensation spreading beneath her thighs.

"Heated seats," Cole said. "We haven't needed them till now."

She wasn't sure they did even then. "Nice feature."

"Great in the winter. Or when you forget your coat."

"Or burn it." She slid down into the seat, luxuriating in the cozy warmth as much as the teasing, the strange twists their relationship had taken.

Twenty minutes later Cole shook his head and rubbed a hand across the lines in his forehead. "I still can't believe I did that."

She laughed. "You looked so horror-stricken."

"I've never set a woman's clothes on fire."

"I believe you."

From the doubtful look on his face she might just as well have said "I love you." She said that next. It was about time.

He took his hand from the wheel to capture hers and settle it against his thigh. "I'm not sure I deserve that."

"In light of recent events?"

"In firelight is more like it. You should be chewing me out royally."

"From the look on your face you were doing a better job than I ever could."

"Forgive me?"

A tiny warning bell sounded in the back of her mind. She knew better than to forgive him too easily. That was the mistake his mother had made with his father. She pretended to consider. "I'll think about it."

He smiled grimly and nodded toward the road. "Fair enough."

All's fair in love and war, she thought. Including little white lies.

"We drove through here when I was ten," Evie declared. "I could spend a month in Yellowstone."

"If we had camping gear, we might." Cole turned the radio down. "After this we cross into Montana. Bozeman will be an hour or so."

"And you lived near . . . ?"

"Three hours north, toward Great Falls."

"I can't wait to see it."

"It'll be sunset by the time we get there."

Then dark. Then another night with Cole. Evie sat up. She had the queer feeling this night would be different. She wouldn't just show him how she loved him, she'd tell him. She had opened the barred door she'd hidden her feelings behind and he hadn't rejected any of them. Instead of running, he'd chosen to share.

A shiver of desire curled through her. Remembering the nights they'd already shared, she could barely imagine how much closer they could get. He'd already touched her in places she'd never dreamed, reached her in ways she'd never opened to other men.

She ran a finger under her collar.

"Hot?"

In a sense. Shaky too. A languid heat was turning her limbs to putty. She reached for the control panel. "Is this still on?"

"I turned the seat heater off half an hour ago. You dozed off for a while there."

"I missed the middle part of the park."

He glanced at her thighs, a speculative male smile curving his lips. "I was wondering what you were dreaming about."

She turned her face very slowly toward him. "I didn't."

"A few words. A few smiles. If I hadn't heard you moan like that before . . ." He let the image trail off.

Evie swallowed.

"Something wrong?"

"I'd like to stretch my legs a minute."

He immediately responded to her request. The

mountain road had a wide shoulder. Snow-dusted pines cast afternoon shadows across it. Evie unhooked her seat belt, climbed out, and combed the hair off her forehead. Thin crystalline air buffeted her cheeks. "I felt a little light-headed there."

"Too much heat."

"Too many dreams."

He came up beside her, his arm fitting neatly around her waist. "Is that my fault?"

She leaned against his chest, her smile troubled, his body sturdy and warm. "I had the weirdest feeling. Something about destiny."

"It's the altitude."

"Maybe I am a little high."

He ran a hand down the slope of her back. "You're with me."

She never wanted to be anywhere else. They were like the only two people on earth, a magnificent mountainous earth. She listened for far-off cars and heard nothing but the gurgling of a stream clattering over rocks.

Cole chucked her chin upward, the better to look into her eyes. "You're groggy."

She shook her head. "I'm in love. It's scary. Who knows what could go wrong?"

"My Evie? A pessimist?"

She loved it when he called her his. "It isn't like me to get worried over nothing. Are you sure you want to do this?"

"Cruise Montana? It's a beautiful state—when people aren't making it ugly."

"It won't be ugly with you there."

He nuzzled her cheek. "I should have said that."

She held on tight. Saying "I love you" for the second time in one day seemed natural and right. She punctuated it with a kiss.

Cole let the simple words scramble his emotions. He'd had less than a week to get used to being in love. She was still working on it. Taking her in his arms, he knew he'd never get over what it felt like to hold her, what gazing into those blue eyes did to him. "You're getting the hang of this love stuff."

"It shouldn't be so hard to say."

"Depends who you say it to." He let her go long enough to reach in the backseat and fetch his coat. He slung it around her shoulders. The sun was behind the mountain; the air laced with early-season snow. "I think you've finally found your man, Miss Mercer."

"Bud will be so proud."

He chuckled. "We'll have some *I told you so*'s to put up with when we get back."

We. Futures. He was counting her as part of his.

Evie hugged the collar of his coat around her, wishing it was his arms. Not sure where the urgency came from, she followed him around the front of the car. She was done with wishing, she wanted to make things come true. "Kiss me?"

He turned, a puzzled, pleased smile on his face. "Honey, I could kiss you all day."

"Just hold me."

He did. His body curved to hers familiarly, possessively. She formed herself to him. "I love you, Cole."

"I love you."

The next morning, heading northeast from Bozeman, Evie stared at the magnificent scenery. She'd let
him drive, knowing they had to proceed at his pace.
"Your father owned ten thousand acres of this? You
must have been rich."

"Land rich," he said.

Rich in everything but love, she realized.

"My aunt inherited it from my mother. She lets it
out to tenants. I didn't want it."

Evie petted his hair, running her fingers through
the sandy strands. Light glinted off the melting snow.
Sun shot through the gold highlights. Although he'd
been narrating a travelogue history of Montana, she'd
sensed his tension the minute they'd woken up.

He hadn't been back in sixteen years. He was on a
mission. She watched the dour expression on his face,
the way memories matched with reality each time they
passed a landmark he remembered.

He nodded to a small ranch. "That's where Maria
and her husband live. Or lived. She was our housekeeper for ten years. Her husband branded cattle for us
every spring. We're getting closer."

Close in more ways than one, Evie thought. He was
taking her where he'd never taken another woman; letting her travel a landscape of scars and bad memories,
sharing the bad with the good.

She said little, taking in as much as she could—
hints, sighs, the meaning of that thin angry line carved
between his brow, the reverence in his eyes when he
peered at a line of mountains. He joked about senti-

mental journeys. She listened for echoes in the pristine valleys. It wasn't easy correlating the vast blue sky with the sound of slaps, the thud of fists. She contrasted the wary gentle man she knew, his dry humor, his sexual passion, with the violent past he'd alluded to. He'd made such sweet love to her the night before. It was almost as if he were making up for something, forestalling something.

They were there now. Together. It would be all right.

She reached for his hand.

He held hers for a moment before returning his grip to the wheel. She rubbed the knot in his neck, stroking the tense muscles. He rolled his head and sighed. "I think I'm more nervous than you," she said with a laugh.

"What is there to worry about?"

What indeed? She watched the road for a few miles, kneading his neck as he drove.

He reached for her hand, splaying her fingers across his chest, his heartbeat a reassuring thump. "The ranch can't hurt you," he said.

"But the past can."

"Yours *and* mine. We've both let the past control who we let in."

"Very true."

"It'll probably look like a house and a few barns. Nothing special. My father always did make sure we kept up appearances. My mother too. It's what goes on underneath you never know about."

Evie believed him. There were times, lying in Cole's arms, when she felt she saw to his soul and back, when every word was honest, unsparing, direct. Then there were moments like this, when he was miles away and all the touches in the world couldn't bridge the gap. It was as if he was hitchhiking some remembered road alone, as isolated and remote as the hills. With no one to turn to, he'd learned to be self-sufficient. She admired that. She respected him for it.

She also wondered if she'd ever get used to it. He wanted her, but would he ever allow himself to need her? He was so used to going it on his own.

She had to be careful not to try to overdo—to volunteer feelings, insights, to give too much. She didn't want to pry. All the same, she wondered what he was thinking.

He hunched his shoulders, temporarily dislodging her hand. She'd been kneading his neck again. "We aren't going much further if you keep doing that."

She set her hands in her lap. Maybe she was going too far already. She tried not to sound defensive. "You looked tense."

"Yeah? I'd call it turned on."

She gaped at him.

He huffed a laugh. "You think you can touch me like that and I won't feel it? Honey, it's all I can do to keep my hands on the wheel."

Flames raced to her cheeks. "I didn't mean to—"

He lowered his voice to a suggestive rasp. "I know. You're sexy as sin without half trying. That only makes it worse."

Her eyes darted to the scenery. It suddenly seemed as pale as a watercolor. "I didn't mean to tease."

"I hope you mean to finish what you started."

"How?"

The crunch of gravel beneath the tires signaled his intentions.

"There's no scenic turnoff here."

"There's a major turn-on. Come here."

"We can't."

'Why not? We haven't passed a car in an hour."

"Cole."

He leaned across the front seat, his arm dangling over the steering wheel, his knee bumping the gearshift. He was as sexy and saucy as a cowboy come to town on a Saturday night. "Think this car's too small for what I have in mind?"

He touched her breast. When she dragged in a breath, he cupped her cheek. She swallowed. That drew his attention to her bare throat. "Altitude making you light-headed again?"

"Could be."

"It wouldn't have anything to do with me, would it?" He lifted her palm to his mouth, laving it with a kiss.

She tried to breathe. "We're in the middle of nowhere."

"I've got all I need."

"What if a policeman comes along?"

"What do you think the chances are of that?"

About the same as her resisting him. "This is crazy."

"I'm surprised we haven't done it before." He shot a look at the messy backseat. "It makes sense, Evie."

"It's high school."

"It could be fun. Take a risk."

She risked melting into his arms every time she let herself get lost in his eyes. "You're a devil, you know that?"

"Kiss me and find out."

ELEVEN

He tugged her sweater from her jeans, the click of the seat belt as loud as a car's backfire. He nipped her earlobe. Her moan was even better. "It won't be anything like the bed last night."

A king-size water bed. She remembered. They'd stretched out, massaging cramped muscles from days in the car, taking turns. She'd memorized every rippling plane of his back. His legs were rangy, sinewy—

She still wasn't sure how they'd get to the backseat. For the moment she was too intent on caressing those same muscles, tracing his shoulder blades to his spine, raking her fingers down his back, feeling the way his thigh bunched when she touched him.

She inhaled sharply. He'd reached up inside her sweater, his hand molding to her breast inside her favorite lacy bra. He'd watched her put it on that morning. The memory sent gooseflesh racing over her body.

She watched his lashes flutter on his cheeks. Eyes closed, he traced the satiny cup with his thumb, tweaking her pebbled nipple, eliciting another moan. He lifted the sweater, dipping his head to her lap, shocking her with a kiss pressed to her navel, the plunging sensation of his tongue.

The snap on her jeans unsnapped. She held her breath. At this rate she wasn't sure they'd make it to the backseat. The idea thrilled her. She loved the way she unhinged him, the sense she got that it took all his willpower to slow down—for her sake. That was love, she thought.

And that, she silently gasped, was a love bite on her neck. "Cole."

He combed her hair off her neck, the better to kiss her again.

Panting, she waited. Lights pulsed behind her closed lids. When he didn't move she stroked her cheek against his, luxuriating in the scent of his skin, the fireworks to come. "Cole?"

He wasn't moving.

She glanced up. He stared over the seat. It dimly occurred to her that the pulsing light hadn't come from behind her eyelids. A police car sat twenty feet from their rear bumper.

She sat up fast. "What ditl we do?"

"Nothing."

She laughed breathlessly, tugging her sweater down. Cole took his place behind the wheel, his face devoid of emotion.

"At least they can't get us for speeding." She chuckled. "Cole?"

"Highway patrol. Don't say anything," he commanded in a flat voice. "Let me do the talking."

She huffed. This was hardly the time for him to turn macho. It was funny, really, having a policeman pull up when they'd been . . . well. She blushed. The patrolman was still in his car, a radio handset to his mouth. "He must be calling in our license plate."

Cole grunted, eyes straight ahead.

"We may have been going a trifle fast, but I don't think they give tickets for that." She laughed again. He'd once said he loved the way her eyes sparkled when she made a joke.

His mouth barely twitched.

An uneasy silence enveloped the car. She put her hand on his arm. "It's okay, Cole."

He raised his hand to halt her. He didn't want to hear it.

She followed his icy gaze to the rearview mirror. The flash of a uniform drew her head around. The policeman strolled up to the driver's window.

Cole pressed the button on the armrest. A gusting wind buffeted the car. Its howl melded with the electronic hum of the window scrolling down.

Standing just behind Cole's door, the trooper leaned on the window ledge. Evie noted the way he subtly crowded his prey. Despite his black sunglasses, she got the distinct feeling she was being minutely inspected too. She didn't blame him. Next to domestic disputes, traffic stops could be the most dangerous part of a policeman's job.

"Got trouble?" he asked.

"Sight-seeing," Cole replied tersely.

The trooper made a show of craning his neck at the

long flat valley and the mountains ringing it. "Not much to see around here."

"It's beautiful," Evie declared. She crouched toward the window, the better to see the trooper's face. "I've never been in Montana."

The trooper smiled faintly. Evie watched her grinning reflection distorted in his black sunglasses.

"And you, sir?"

Cole muttered something.

"Pardon me?" The trooper leaned in so close, his face was almost even with Cole's.

"I've seen it."

Thick fingers tapped the door while he considered. "Could I see your license, please? Sir?"

Evie's smile felt plastered to her face. She wanted to prod Cole, make him move a little faster.

The policeman spoke again. "Just routine, sir."

Cole fished his wallet from his back pocket. When he leaned forward the trooper straightened. Evie caught a glimpse of the gun strapped to his hip, its butt end covered with dull black leather.

Cole slid out his license and handed it over.

"This your current address, sir?"

"Yes."

"And you, ma'am?"

"I'm from Michigan too. I've got my license here somewhere." She reached for the backseat.

"No need," the policeman said. He turned and strolled back to his car.

Evie waited until his was out of earshot. "You could be a little more polite."

Cole stared straight ahead, his face stony. "Why?"

"For all he knows, we broke down."

"I hope that's all he knows."

"What does that mean?"

Cole's hand tightened on the wheel. He glanced at the mirror again. For a second she got the uneasy feeling he was thinking of taking off, racing for the Canadian border.

She forced another laugh. "I am of age, you know."

He barely smiled at her strained humor. He ran a hand over his mouth, pulling his cheeks taut. Then he noticed her watching, a worried look creasing her brow. He reached for her hand and squeezed it. "Sorry. You hitchhike across the country, and you don't always have good experiences with cops."

"They hassled you?"

"More than once. Some of them gave me a ride or bought me something to eat. They're not all bad."

Then why couldn't he keep his eyes off that mirror?

She laughed. It came out more genuine this time. "Hey, maybe that restaurant owner is after us. You know, setting fire to personal property. Arson?"

"Very funny."

"I'll visit you in jail."

"Cute, Mercer."

"Honest. I'll wear a veil and we'll talk on telephones through chicken-wire glass. I'll be there every day."

"I bet you would."

"I'd bake a cake with a file in it."

"Cut it out."

He wasn't kidding. The policeman sauntered up to

the driver's side window. His sunglasses draped from his shirt pocket. He looked less intimidating that way.

Evie breathed a sigh of relief. It was obvious that being questioned got Cole's hackles up. In a sense she couldn't blame him. However, there was enough macho posturing going on without making it worse.

"Be polite," she whispered.

The trooper angled himself toward the front of the car this time, the better to see Cole's face. "Did you say you lived around here?"

"I said I'd been here."

He pointed at Cole's chest. "Aren't you Chris Raynes?"

Cole said nothing.

"Didn't you go to McKinley High? Class of eighty? Eighty-two? No, wait. Did you graduate?"

Cole looked up just long enough to register a face he'd long since recognized.

Evie felt a cool shudder race across her skin.

The trooper whipped his hat off. A wide grin took ten years off his face. "Rob Kittridge. I was a couple years behind you."

"I don't remember."

"We were in track together. Of course, I was JV. You lettered four years running. Ha. Running, track. Get it?"

Cole said nothing.

Kittridge idly rubbed his thumb across the license in his hand. "I thought the name sounded familiar. I mean, there's a Cole Creek that runs just south of your family's ranch, right?"

"You got it."

He settled his hat back on, the visor shining black patent leather. He handed over the license. Cole slid it into his wallet.

Evie's head spun. From the trooper's hearty tone she'd expected a reunion of some kind. Sure, he had the name wrong, but she knew Cole recognized him. She saw it in his troubled eyes. "Cole." She nudged him. "Cole, he's talking to you."

Kittridge laughed again. "Come on out here. Let me look at you."

Cole looked at her instead. She felt her encouraging smile stiffen. "What is it?"

The trooper's jocular tone of voice changed slightly. "I said come on out here."

"Is there anything else you need?" Cole asked.

Evie watched the trooper's gaze fall to Cole's hands —occupied with the wallet. He put his meaty hand on the door handle. "Could you step out of the car, sir?"

She sat forward. "Oh, this is silly." It was like two bulldogs circling each other for a fight.

The door handle clicked.

Cole stiffened then stepped out. The same height as the policeman, he lacked the younger man's beefy build. He slid the wallet in his back pocket.

"Could you put your hands on the car, sir?"

Evie craned her neck toward the window. "What is going on here?"

Cole turned. All she saw was his belt buckle, his chest, his elbows when he raised his arms to set them on the roof. Her stomach turned over when the policeman patted him down.

"Why the alias?" Kittridge asked.

"It isn't an alias. It's mine."

"Clearly there's some misunderstanding here," Evie insisted. "You're confusing him with someone else."

"Is your real name Christopher Raynes?"

"It was."

She felt as if an icicle had formed around her spine. She tried to catch a glimpse of Cole's face. Instead, just beyond him, she saw the policeman take the catch off his holster.

She scooted across the seat toward the door.

"Please stay inside, miss."

"I have a right to know what's going on here."

The trooper drew his gun.

Her heart lodged in her throat.

The officer calmly gave Cole a series of commands. "Hands behind your head. Link your fingers. Now step away from the car. Slowly. Spread-eagle." He gestured at the pavement with a flick of his wrist. The gun barrel glinted dully.

Cole grazed it with a look then raked the mountains with a long stare. The trooper gestured again. Cole dropped to his knees.

"Stop this," Evie cried. "You leave him alone." She pushed at the door.

The trooper held it closed. "Stay there, miss."

"What are you doing to him?" She couldn't look. She couldn't see the man she loved facedown on the road, his cheek pressed to the asphalt, fingers linked on the back of his head as if he were a criminal.

Blocking her view, the trooper leaned in the window. She sat back.

"It's for your own protection, miss. There are out-standing warrants on this man."

"Outstanding? For what? His name's Cole Creek. He's a mechanic. He lives in Michigan. He's on assignment with me for a magazine called *Consumers'*—"

"He's wanted for murder, miss."

She stopped. Time stopped. Every detail of the trooper's uniform came into knife-edged focus. "What?"

"His real name is Christopher Michael Raynes. He's wanted for murder in Montana."

The highway patrol station was a joke, a prefab building on a corner lot in a tiny town at the foot of a mountain. It looked like a temporary school building, a credit-union branch office. Evie pulled into the parking lot, her hands clammy and clamped to the wheel. She'd followed Kittridge's car all the way, her gaze focused on Cole's silhouette in the backseat. He never turned around.

Before Kittridge's car had coasted to a stop, two officers emerged from the makeshift building to escort Cole inside.

Evie wanted to throw the Conquest in park and race after him. She sat there, unmoving, her heart an aching hole in her chest, her breath wheezing in and out of her lungs.

She forced the door open. The thin mountain air felt like lead. She moved as if underwater. Shouldering her way through the front door, she sensed the hubbub of conversation die instantly. Four police officers turned to look at her.

She looked at the room. The inside was no more impressive than the outside, cheap wood paneling, gray indoor/outdoor carpet. There were three desks in the reception area. A cubicle divider covered with calendars and family photos gave the back two some privacy from each other. The front desk sat off to the left.

She walked up to it, ignoring the other patrolmen. She waited for the man to get off the telephone. He took his time.

"May I help you?"

"I'm with Cole Creek. I'd like to talk to him."

A middle-aged man with a paunch and a road map of wrinkles, he quirked his mouth in a sneer and glanced at the new paperwork on his desk. "No one by that name here."

"He just came in—" The futility almost swamped her. She rallied for Cole's sake. "You may have him under another name."

"Did he tell you that?"

"I only know him as Cole Creek. That's his name. There's been a mistake."

The officer reached for a legal pad. He indicated an orange plastic chair with his pen. "Care to tell us about it?"

She sat. "He's done nothing wrong."

"Not according to our records." Despite the harshness of his words, his tone had gentled.

Evie had the feeling she could talk to him. The smirking policemen behind her didn't care; they didn't know Cole. "I know there's been a mistake, Sergeant. Somehow. Someway."

He grimaced then motioned his colleagues from the room. "Call me Dornan. And tell me what you know about Cole Creek."

"Can I see him?"

"We have to ask him some questions."

They'd been doing that for half an hour. Every time there was a pause in her conversation with Dornan, Evie turned toward the short hall that led to the other half of the building. She imagined a maze of small offices and dead-end hallways. She imagined Cole in a bleak room behind a table littered with Styrofoam cups and ashtrays. Kind of like Dornan's desk.

"I think that's all the information we need," Dornan said, entering the last of her comments in a computer. A fax unscrolled in the corner. Before it had finished, one of the other policemen emerged from the back and ripped it off.

"You said I could see him."

Dornan glanced up. "There are a few things you might want to know first."

She braced herself.

"Your boyfriend is wanted for murder, unlawful flight, assault with intent, and a handful of other charges associated with not answering a warrant."

"When? How? He's been in Michigan the last two years. I can vouch for him."

"This was sixteen years ago."

"You mean when he was sixteen?" She stared at the

floor. Cole had made no pretense of loving his father. He'd said he'd hit him. She remembered the long pause before he'd admitted that much.

She shook her head. "That was years ago. Isn't there a statute of limitations?"

"Not on murder. However, we don't have all the facts yet. When we're done questioning him we have to send him to Bozeman to be processed."

"What does that mean? Who do I talk to? Is there a phone here? Don't I get a phone call?"

He laughed, more fatherly than she'd expected. "You're not under arrest here, Ms. Mercer. You can call anyone you like." He nodded toward a pay phone.

Her hand shook as she fed her credit card into it. She stared at the buttons. Who could she call? They were two thousand miles from home. But Cole *was* home. If that was his name.

It was a waking nightmare. The one person she wanted to talk to was Cole. And she wasn't even sure she knew him.

She took a chair by the walnut paneling. Two hours passed. More faxes arrived. More phones rang. Kittridge came in to brag and accept congratulations. "I took one look and knew I remembered him. I pretended to call in his license. Instead of asking for Creek, I asked Dornan what we had on that old Chris Raynes thing—" He noticed Evie and stopped.

She rested her head against the wall. No one had talked to her since Dornan. She prayed she'd answered his questions correctly. Either way they'd been satisfied that she was uninvolved.

She closed her eyes and pressed her lips together. She was as involved as a woman could be. She loved him.

But did she know him? Or had she made the worst mistake of her life? Seeing what she wanted to see, believing what she wanted to believe. She couldn't dwell on that now. A burst of static on the police scanner jerked her attention back to the office, a patrolman radioing in a routine traffic stop, license verification requested.

A few hours earlier she and Cole had been just another couple on the road, undergoing the same procedure.

Not Cole. Christopher, she thought, unable to make the name fit the face.

The hall door opened. Her heart skipped. Cole emerged, walking between two officers. She couldn't have said how she got to her feet or how many steps separated them. All she knew was that one minute she sat, the next she was there, longing to lay her hand on his chest, to put her arms around his neck.

The officers fell back. Try as she might, she couldn't bridge the distance.

He looked smaller between the two hefty men, his face narrower, his eyes sharper than a hawk's. His gaze never left her face. "You're still here," he said.

She'd thought of so many things to say. That she loved him. That she'd get him out of this. Other words tumbled out first. "What's going on? Cole, tell me there's been a mistake."

She couldn't pierce the shielded, shamed look in his eyes. He looked furious. He looked guilty. "Go home, Evie."

She hadn't even checked into a hotel. She didn't know where she'd be staying. She just knew she wasn't going. "I'm not leaving here without you."

"Go."

The word bounced off her. She stepped closer, her gaze boring into his. "What's your name?"

The bleakness in his eyes almost cut her in two. "Cole Creek."

"It's Christopher Raynes," one of the officers corrected.

"I chose it," Cole said. "I swore I'd never use his name again."

"Your father's?"

"I left it all behind."

"He fled," another officer said. "There was a warrant with his name on it."

"That was three days after I left the state," he snapped. "I didn't even know he was dead until I reached Nebraska."

Evie didn't know what to say. She didn't know what he'd told them. She didn't want to mess up his story.

She straightened her spine, realizing what she was thinking. The man she loved would have told the truth. There was no need to protect him from that.

But he lied to you about his name, a small voice said.

She spoke directly to Cole. "You told me it took six months for you to work your way from Texas to Nebraska."

"That's true. When I got to Nebraska there was a letter from my mother saying my father was dead."

"You killed him," Kittridge said, elbowing his way into the conversation.

"He was beating up my mother. I hit him."

"For the last time."

"I had to stop him."

"Permanently?"

"I hit him. He went down. He wasn't dead when I left."

"He had a heart attack three days later," Kittridge said. "The prosecutor claimed it was directly linked to the beating you gave him."

"I hit him once."

"And the trauma led to the heart attack. Assault is a crime."

"Then why didn't you ever arrest him for what he did to my mother?"

Kittridge straightened. "Killing someone in the course of committing any crime is felony murder."

"I didn't give him a heart attack."

"That's for the jury to decide."

"Not much of a case," Dornan muttered.

Evie longed to thank the older man for that much. She couldn't stop looking at Cole. So many silent words passed between them. Her look begged him to tell her the truth. Having to ask was killing her. Worse than all of it was the self-disgust on his face, the guilt.

"Shouldn't we go?" he asked the officer to his left.

"No." Her cry startled everyone.

He stopped in the door, his shoulders as tense as if she'd just plunged a knife in them.

"I love you."

"Don't."

Shards of ice pierced her chest. She knew what she had to say. It didn't matter that she'd joked about it only hours ago. "I'll get the best lawyers. I've called Bud, and Michael, my editor. We'll do everything we can. I'll visit you—"

"Every day?" His quiet sneer cut her to the quick. She'd never seen such coldness in his eyes.

She wasn't letting him push her away. "Yes, I will."

"I'm not the man for you, Evie. I never was."

TWELVE

Evie sat on the bed of another motel, this one on the edge of the road they'd taken back into Bozeman. Another beige room, empty without Cole. How many nights had they shared? Three? Four? How could she have come to love him so deeply so fast?

How could she have been so blind?

She tried everything to quiet the nagging *I told you so* in the back of her mind. She'd read into his silences, misinterpreting them as gentleness, self-sufficiency. He didn't need to make idle chatter. Didn't need small talk. The few words he said, he meant.

He didn't even tell you his real name.

How could she have been so gullible? Again?

She wanted to lie back on the bed and cry. She imagined tears stinging the inside of her eyelids, scalding her cheeks as they ran back into her hair, dampening the pillow with its scratchy pillowcase.

She didn't move. She sat and stared at the highway and the mountains beyond. A semi roared by. A camper plodded along behind it. Happy people, vacationers, sightseers.

She saw nothing but the caged look in Cole's eyes when they'd taken him into the jail. He was sixteen all over again, back in the hell he'd escaped twice. He wouldn't escape a third time. He was still paying for his father's crimes.

"Stop it." Her voice surprised her. She looked around the room, at the TV screen's blank gray face. She would not romanticize him. Wasn't that at the root of all her troubles? She had to face facts, to learn the truth. To do that she needed to talk to him.

He'd told her not to visit.

Tough. She would not sit by and make up motives for him, assume, infer, go over every conversation they'd ever had for clues, hints, insinuations. People said things; did they have any idea how many ways they could be interpreted?

She knew. In the last few hours she'd gone over every glance, every touch, every hesitation.

She'd gone back to the very beginning. She'd thought at the time that he'd held her hand a second too long when he'd first shaken it. He'd looked her in the eye as if he saw something special there. She'd felt a tug on her heart, a spark of undeniable chemistry.

She covered her face with her hands. "Stop it. He looked at you. That's it." They'd shaken hands. He'd gone and washed his. It was pitiful to read the beginnings of true love into that.

Look at what she'd done next! Calling a psychic. Was that desperation or what? Whatever gave her the idea she'd overcome her tendency to believe any man who gave her the time of day?

"You are not a desperate woman. You're intelligent, funny, caring." She was a lot of things. And never more so than when she was with Cole.

She wrapped her arms around her middle, remembering the hunger in his eyes, the strength in his arms when he'd held her. Armies couldn't have torn them apart.

The police had.

She hung her head. What had the psychic said? They were on a journey together. "Look where it led." She was sitting in a motel just down the road from the jail. Mountains hemmed her in. Bars hemmed him in.

The very thought of Cole in a cell made her moan. She rocked back and forth, her head pounding.

The worst part was, he'd tried to tell her. She saw that now. He'd told her he was no good; they weren't right for each other; he'd hated his father.

She hadn't listened.

But murder? She couldn't even bring herself to say the word. "Self-defense." That sounded better. But was that just more wishful thinking?

She launched herself off the bed and strode to her suitcase. She pulled out the laptop, found a legal pad, and started writing things out in longhand.

Murder made no sense. Not the man she knew.

Or thought you knew.

"Know," she insisted. "And love." She loved him. That was the only true thing she could rely on. Yes, other men had fooled her. But she wasn't caving in this time. She believed in herself, in her judgment, in her instincts. She loved this man because he was gentle, honorable, committed, decent. He'd overcome horrendous odds to become the man he was today.

She flipped the page and started a new list: *Self-Defense.* Killing in self-defense was only legal if one's own life was in danger. She knew that much. If he had killed his father to protect his mother, he'd have a real battle ahead of him.

"But he tried to extricate himself," she argued. "He ran away. The authorities hauled him back. What else could he do? He had to fight, for his mother, for himself."

She remembered what he'd said about being beaten black-and-blue after that first escape. There had to be evidence. Medical records. Witnesses. Teachers. Coaches. Boys who ran track wore shorts. Did the bruises show?

She jumped up to find a telephone directory, blinking at how dark the room had become. Hours had passed as she plotted her strategy.

Cole wouldn't approve of what she was about to do. It didn't matter. She loved him. Not blindly but thoroughly. She was going into this with pages of questions in search of answers. And, like any good consumer reporter, she was going to dig for them.

"My dad rarely ever raised his voice. Except—" Evie paused. Sitting at a picnic table beside the road, she smiled fondly, squinting into the distance in the desert sun.

"Except?" Cole asked.

"Dad's semiannual housecleaning project. Changing

storm windows could turn the sweetest Jekyll into a raging Hyde. Watching him work on household projects is where I learned to cuss."

"Butternuts?"

"Worse. Of course it drove Mom around the bend. 'Don't you use that language in front of our daughter,' she'd say."

Cole laughed. "Amateurs. Nothing compared to mine."

"No?"

Cole turned over on his bunk. He drove his fist into his pillow and shoved it against the iron bedframe. Why did he torture himself with memories? Little things. A smile. A snatch of conversation. A bantering argument in the car over radio stations, snacks, travel routes.

He touched his bare feet to the cement floor, gripping the thin mattress. She hadn't come to see him. He'd told her not to. At the time he'd been sure she'd ignore him. Nothing scared Evie away.

Except the truth.

He shut his eyes until pinpricks of light danced behind them. He paced. He knew this cell by heart. It had been three days. How far would she be by now? Iowa? Illinois? She might even be home.

He'd been cruel, telling her to leave. Hell, he'd been scared—and gut-wrenching, skin-crawling afraid she'd see it and love him less.

He'd hidden it the way he hid bruises as a teen. He had put on the rusty armor he'd developed long ago, the "I don't care" shield he wore every time his dad had hit him. "You can't hurt me if I don't let you." He'd absorbed every blow.

He would learn to live with this one.

He had no business loving a woman like Evie. They were worlds apart—her with her loving family, him with his past.

He hadn't murdered his father. He'd sure as hell wanted to.

He braced his arm against the wall, leaning his forehead to the tile until the cold cleared his head. He deserved this. For being a bad son. For never having been able to defend his mother. He'd begged her to leave the man she loved. She'd told him she couldn't. So he'd left *her*—and blamed himself for it ever after.

Was it ever possible to leave the people you loved?

He didn't know. Had Evie left him?

He spun toward the barred door. A clank at the end of the hall faded. The unforgivable part was that he'd hurt her the way his father had hurt the woman he claimed to love. Only Cole had been subtler about it. He'd used words, not fists.

He remembered the pain on her face, the questions in her eyes. He tortured himself with memories of a woman he shouldn't have loved, all the times he shouldn't have touched her. He remembered the way her skin glowed in the morning, the way he smoothed suds over her in the shower, her body glistening, her voice echoing in the confined space, laughing, teasing, soft mews of pleasure, groans of pure desire.

He remembered his mouth buried against her neck, her hands turning to jelly on the steering wheel. They'd been driving through Arizona, leaving the Grand Canyon, heading for another night together.

"Stop that," she'd commanded.

"Keep your eye on the road and your foot on the gas."

"And your hands to yourself, Creek."

He'd put his hands in his lap. And his lips on her neck.

She'd quivered. He'd touched her hair, her ear, tracing it, watching her lips part, dragging in air. Her tongue darted out to wet those lips.

"I never thought—" She lost the thought.

He'd stolen it. Just like he'd stolen her love. From that first day he'd waited and watched and told himself no and gone after her anyway. He'd kissed her their first night together. He'd kissed her a hundred times after. It would never be enough to get him through the years to come.

It would have to do. He hoarded the images. The way she swallowed when he ran his finger down her silky throat. The way she leaned, against her will, toward his hand, her lids fluttering to half-mast.

The iron bedframe squeaked, his fist clenched around it. He'd cupped the back of her head in his palm, her hair filtering through his fingers in deep brown-and-chestnut strands. She'd arched back, angling beside the headrest so she could open her neck to his next hungry kiss.

Hungry? He'd been starving. Her dress's buttons had stretched taut across her breasts when she arched. He'd undone one button, then two. He'd reached inside. Her leg came up, her knee bumping the steering wheel. "I'm driving," she'd murmured.

"Don't stop."

A short pant, a gasp. "I think that's my line."

He'd felt the car slow. So did he. Lifting her dress, he'd slid his hand between her thighs, slick with sweat, indescribably sweet smelling. He'd caressed her until they were both dizzy with wanting.

"I'm going to run off the road," she protested weakly.

He'd moved his hand to her breast, measuring the rapid pump of her heart versus the pound of his. His thumb grazed her nipple. "Find a place."

"Give me a minute."

"Baby, I'll give you hours."

She'd tried to laugh. He'd tried to control himself. That night they'd made love until their bodies were coated in sweat, their flesh quivering and exhausted. He'd never loved her more.

Back in the cell, he slammed his palm against the wall. Liar. He loved her more than ever. That's why he'd sent her away. That's why he'd sell his soul to have her visit him. Just once. "No."

He rubbed his tired eyes until they ached. He scraped his hand across the back of his neck. The last thing he wanted was to see the look in her eyes when she said she loved him. He didn't want her loving him in that total, life-destroying way his mother clung to. Which brought him back to the matter at hand.

He hadn't killed his father. He sighed at how tired the words seemed. Yes, he'd wanted him dead. He was being punished for the desire if not the deed. The irony was that his father had *taught* him to strike out. So he had. He'd hit back. Eventually it had caught up with him.

Some things you didn't outrun. Family. Destiny.

He rubbed his eyes again. Hadn't Evie asked him about destiny once? Their first night out. Some psychic on the radio. He chased the memory away. He didn't need a fortune-teller telling him what came next. Evie was gone. It was better that way. He'd tell himself that until the day he died.

"You've got a visitor."

Evie heard the guard's words echo down the corridor. She waited. Doors slammed. Others slid into place. The visiting room was depressingly banal; gray-and-green linoleum, painted cement-block walls. Fluorescent lights buzzed overhead. Tables and chairs were set up in four groupings. She'd never been in a jail before. She suspected they all looked exactly the same.

A door opened at the far end of the room. She lowered her gaze to her briefcase while the guard escorted Cole to the table. "I asked to see you."

He spread his hands as if to say, "Here I am."

She heard the handcuffs clink and looked up. His shirt was a dingy gray hospital scrub worn tunic style over jeans. The V neck revealed a scattering of chest hair. She stared at the handcuffs looped through a heavy brown belt sagging at his waist. Had he lost weight?

Her legs threatened to buckle. She sat down.

He hesitated then did the same, dragging out a blue plastic chair. "I thought you'd gone home."

She lowered her briefcase as if it were glass and might shatter. Her hands shook too much to undo the combination lock. She folded them in her lap and looked him in the eye. Hollow cheeks. Stark cheekbones. Flat blue eyes with a wary "stay back" look. He wasn't letting her near him.

"I don't know what to call you. Christopher. Chris?"

"Try Cole."

"Your real name *is* Christopher Raynes."

"I chose Cole Creek when I left home. I wanted a fresh start."

"I don't blame you for that."

"But you can for everything else."

"You mean you think I should."

"Don't make excuses for me, Evie."

"I've been finding out the truth."

"That I did everything they've accused me of?"

"You didn't kill him."

"I hit him. Then I ran away."

"You were sixteen."

"I don't know if knocking him out caused his heart attack or not. To tell you the truth, when I heard he was dead I was surprised he'd a heart to attack him. I was glad, Evie."

She knew he was trying to shock her, to play it tough. The effort it took him broke her heart. She folded her hands on the table beside her case. "You gave a man a heart attack three days *after* you left the state."

"I'd wanted him dead for years."

"So you've said."

"I lied."

She looked up.

"To you, Evie."

"About your name."

"About everything."

"I don't believe it."

He slapped the table. The guard looked over.

Evie didn't flinch. "I've been thinking over everything you said. Everything we did. I can't be *that* gullible, Cole. I know love when I feel it."

The smell of a nearby ashtray wafted toward them, sooty, sickening. Cole slid it nearer then shoved it away. He wished to heaven he had a cigarette. "You don't know what you feel."

"I do."

"Can't you see this is what love does to women? It makes them blind—"

The guard coughed into his fist.

Cole had leaned forward, urgent and intense. His knees almost bumped hers under the table. His hands had reached out without him realizing it. The cuff chain scraped the edge of the table. He sat back, shoulders slumped.

"Dammit, Evie. Listen to me. Look at me. Is this what you want? I'm not the man you thought I was. I lied about my name, my past—"

"From everything I've learned, you were very honest on that account."

"Then listen to this. I'm not right for you. Have the sense to walk away. Now."

"I love you."

"Don't. And don't look at me that way. Don't love me as if everything I've ever done is okay."

"You had a rotten childhood."

"Oh yeah. Nothing was my fault. It was my temper not me."

"Dammit, Cole, I am not your mother. She stood up for a monster in the name of defending the man she loved. I'm standing up for a kid who couldn't fight back, for a man who made something of his life."

"So you want to believe. But then it's easy to fool you, isn't it?"

She sat back. "You go for a person's weak spot when you want to win, don't you?"

Cole ground his wrist against the table's edge. He felt like a heel. No matter how he wanted to apologize, he couldn't. If he caved now, he'd drag her into his arms, beg her to believe in him. And she would.

He worked his jaw, glaring at the table's peeling walnut veneer. He closed his eyes and dragged in a slow breath graced with a hint of her perfume. It was as if she was inside him, curling around his heart, tightening like barbed wire. He had to send her away.

The softest whisper of a touch grazed his fist. His face hardened, a ragged exhale escaped. He slowly opened his eyes.

She'd moved her briefcase to the side, the better to shield the guard's view.

They had to keep arguing, to prevent him noticing anything had changed. "Don't look at me like that," Cole said, his tone roughened by doubt.

"I've been talking to your lawyer."

"Court-appointed." He sneered. His thumb scudded across her knuckles.

"I called Celine Connors. She's a crackerjack criminal attorney."

"Is that what I am?"

Her fingers twined through his. "She thinks there's a good chance you'll get out of this without a trial. The charge is old, barely substantiated. The prosecutor who brought it originally—" Her gaze strayed to her briefcase.

Cole drew a finger along her pulse. He had to remind himself to play at disdain. "The prosecutor knew my father. They were hunting buddies."

"He's retired now. The new man is less interested in protecting the powers that be and more in favor of the underdog. He's a crusader, a liberal—"

"Then you two should get along fine."

"Cole."

He wanted her too much to hold on any longer. He released her hand.

Her gaze wavered, her lashes blinking rapidly. She slid the case between them and opened it. The lid formed a barrier between them and the guard.

Too obvious. The guard wandered over and peered over the top. Nothing but papers inside. He glanced at their hands, separated by the table. Cole linked his fingers tightly before him. The guard strolled back to his spot by the door.

Cole clenched one fist inside the other. "It's over, Evie."

She refused to listen. That was his fault too. He never should have touched her, never given in.

She pulled out a notebook. Yellow this time. "Let me explain my methodology."

He snorted. He should have known. His Evie wasn't one to back down when challenged.

"I decided to do what any consumer researcher would do. I called four attorneys. I interviewed each, asking for references, word of mouth, a list of satisfied and dissatisfied customers. I called the state bar—"

She was on a roll, flipping the pages of her new notebook. "Okay, so, Celine Connors—she's your lawyer now."

"And the one the court appointed?"

"You refused to talk to him."

He'd been a scruffy law-school grad who'd whipped in, got Cole's name wrong three times in a row, then disappeared when Cole told him what he could do with his strategy. "He wanted me to plead."

"Plead guilty?"

"He said it'd be easier than a trial."

Evie swallowed the knot in her throat. "You didn't consider it."

"Maybe I killed my father, maybe I didn't. I can't regret it, Evie."

"You know you didn't kill him," she declared hotly.

"It doesn't matter. I won't plead."

She heaved a sigh of relief. "At least you're not totally crazy."

He was for loving her. He thought of what a trial would do to her. She'd never give up. She'd fight to the bitter end. His father had been a powerful man, well respected. Although Cole had gotten hints that people sympathized with what he and his mother endured, no one had ever stepped forward and stopped it. The stand-alone, settler mentality ran strong in Montana.

"A trial could take months," he said. "If they find me guilty—"

"They won't. Besides, there are appeals."

There was also the death penalty in this state. Neither one of them mentioned it.

"You don't want to be here, Evie."

She shrugged, pulling out another sheaf of papers. "Too late. I am."

"Then I don't want you here." He leaned forward and grasped both her hands in his. "Don't throw your life away on me."

The guard said his name.

He let go as if burned.

Evie continued. "Celine's first tactic is to press the statute of limitations."

"It doesn't apply to murder."

"One charge at a time. She's collecting every bit of evidence she can on your background. As for me, I've assembled a list of people who will attest to your character since you left Montana. Your present employer, past employers, your commanding officer in the army."

He listened in silence as thick as the cement walls, his eyes as blue as those skies cutting between the flinty mountain peaks.

"We've both interviewed former ranch hands, your housekeeper Maria, former teachers, your high-school coach. They're giving depositions regarding years of abuse, corroborating the way you tried to protect your mother."

"And failed."

She continued with her list of potential witnesses. "That old girlfriend of yours, the one you dated for a while in high school. She had a lot to say."

"I'll bet."

Cole watched. She was unswervable, all right. The more he saw her throwing her life away on his account, the more he saw how his mother must have started, bright-eyed and in love, refusing to believe the worst.

He knew what he had to do. He'd do it right this time.

"That's it," she concluded brightly.

"Are you done?"

"We're only starting—"

"What about your job?"

"You became an employee of the magazine when you agreed to come with me. An independent contractor, maybe, but Michael has said he'd be willing to give me some time to help you out—"

He got up, shoving the chair back. "Visit's over."

The guard pushed himself off the wall as Cole strode toward him. Ten steps and he'd be gone. The click on her briefcase made him flinch. He clenched his jaw.

"I'm not giving up," she announced.

"Go home."

"I'll be at the hearing Friday."

"Don't."

"Cole."

He turned in the doorway. The blood seemed to have drained from his face. His shoulders wouldn't raise up no matter how he tried. He felt beaten down. He didn't like how familiar that felt. Sixteen years earlier he would've given anything to have someone on his side. He couldn't do that to her now.

His voice barely carried across the room. "What do

I have to do, plead guilty? Get this over with so you'll go home and forget about me?"

He saw the fear in her eyes, the doubt flickering across her face as she tried to find the words. Did she defy him and make him *more* stubborn? Or did she acquiesce? A voice shouted in his head, *Say no. Tell me you'll stay*. He killed it.

"Go home, Evie. I don't need your help or your lawyers or your research. Don't wait for me. I won't be waiting for you."

THIRTEEN

The courtroom smelled like carpet glue and new wool. The rows of seats smelled of oil soap. Evie looked at the circular window behind the gallery. The sun shone through it, casting a circle of light high on the wall over the jury box. It moved in tiny stages like a sundial. Evie counted the minutes.

She rose when the bailiff ordered them to rise and sat when her legs wouldn't hold her anymore. Cole was led in for the preliminary hearing. He wore khakis and a deep green pullover sweater. Celine told her he'd refused to wear a suit.

He took his place behind the table. Celine Connors extended her hand importantly. This was a man to respect, her gesture implied, a valued client.

He hesitated. Out of sheer reluctant politeness, he shook her hand. She whispered something in his ear, her hand patting him on the back.

They turned as the judge entered. "This is a preliminary hearing to establish if there is sufficient grounds for these charges."

Celine was on her feet. Taking the prosecutor by surprise, she asked to approach the bench.

Evie sat in the back row, clutching her purse, trying to see past heads to his sandy hair. He'd slept on it wrong. She recognized the cowlick. She absently rubbed her fingers together, remembering reaching across the car to caress the back of his head.

"He'll be fine," Bud said, leaning forward.

She looked at her old family friend.

Vivian reached across her husband to take Evie's hand. "Everything's going to be okay."

She wished she could believe that. What if he was changing his plea? What if he'd chosen to plead guilty? She craned her neck, straining to catch anything Celine said.

The woman attorney walked back to her table and pulled a list from her briefcase.

Evie couldn't stay. She felt dizzy, nauseated. Like a magnifying glass burning ants, the circular sun had been reduced to a pinprick over the witness stand. She had to get some air.

Celine Connors called Agatha Peterson to the stand. Cole's Aunt Aggie related the few hints her sister had relayed concerning abuse. Her hair frosted, her suit pristine, the elderly woman spoke briskly and to the point, her voice turning flinty when she recalled the first time her nephew arrived on her doorstep, a cold and shivering thirteen-year-old. Her shoulders stiffened when she recounted how she'd called her sister to inform her that Christopher was all right. Her brother-in-law had taken the telephone from his wife. Two days later two men had arrived to take Christopher home.

"What did your sister say after her son was returned to her?" Celine asked.

"Very little."

"And by that you inferred?"

"Objection, Your Honor. Inferences?"

The judge waved it away. "We'll decide admissibility for the real trial. This is just a hearing."

Aggie nodded at his wisdom. "My sister told me what she could. Her silences said as much as her words. Add to that, her husband wouldn't let her talk too long on the telephone. She told me Christopher was home, they were fine, and I shouldn't trouble myself about it again. I offered to come visit for Easter, which was right around the corner."

"And your sister said?"

"Not to bother. It was her way of warning me off."

"Thank you."

"Maria, do you remember any instances of abuse, suspected or seen?"

"Suspected, Your Honor?" The prosecutor was on his feet. "Is this to establish facts or fancies?"

Evie's heart was in her throat. The next day was as grueling as the first, so much hung on each person's testimony.

"In that case, please tell us only what you saw first-hand," Celine said.

The family housekeeper drew a picture of a cowering mother, a son who stepped forward anytime he sensed trouble brewing, an intimidating father who kept his family virtual prisoners on their isolated ranch. "She'd never confide in me. She acted like it was disloyal to say a bad word. I told her all men weren't like that. A pretty woman like her—she could go somewhere, take her son, start over."

"Did she?"

"No. She got him out of the house, though, as much as she could. I can't remember all the times she talked to her husband about signing the boy up for band, sports, any activity that would keep him at school longer every day, give him a chance at a real life."

Evie watched Cole's head lift. She'd gotten a seat on the far right, the better to see his profile. He'd never turned to see her; he was in this alone. All the same, she sensed he'd never looked at his life that way. A parade of former acquaintances had come forward to say they knew, they sympathized. They, too, had been helpless to stop it. That didn't mean they didn't care. Trapped as he was in a family nightmare, Evie suspected Cole had never seen a different side of the picture. She wished she could talk to him about it, just touch him, hold his hand.

He'd refused all visitors.

At the end of three days the judge called a halt to the witnesses, teachers, pastors, school friends. Celine waved stacks of depositions. She gestured to the rows of spectators, claiming she could get a hundred people to testify to the abuse one Christopher Raynes, now known as Cole Creek, had suffered at the hands of his father. Unable to find support in the community, he'd been driven to strike back. Only once. As for his father's heart condition, they'd found the doctor who'd treated him in Helene. A preexisting heart condition could have killed him anytime.

As for Cole's subsequent history, he'd been an exemplary citizen. She had witnesses to testify to that too —employers, friends, customers—people who'd flown two thousand miles on his behalf.

Bud and Vivian sat up straighter.

Cole lowered his head.

Evie watched in tense silence. She'd seen every move, every time he ran his finger under his collar or shifted in his chair. There weren't many of them. The only overt reaction she'd seen occurred at the end of his aunt's testimony.

"Yes, my sister informed me when my brother-in-law died." The older woman had puffed out her chest, reaching into her purse for a tissue. "I'm sorry. It was the hardest thing she ever did."

"And to what do you refer?" Celine asked.

"She sent a letter. In case Chris showed up at my house again. It contained a note she wanted me to give him, telling him never to come home. She thought, once he heard his father was dead, he'd come right back. She didn't want him knowing."

"Knowing what?"

"That people blamed him for it. One person did. That prosecutor. No one else did."

"There were warrants out for his arrest. Why wouldn't she let you tell him?"

"Because she knew he'd want to come home and face up to them. He's always been like that, taking responsibility, carrying the world on his shoulders."

His aunt dabbed her eyes and steadied her voice. Cole hung his head.

His aunt's voice quavered then recovered. "For twelve years she didn't see her boy. For his sake, she let him think she didn't want him. It was the last way she knew to protect him."

Cole balanced his forehead on his fingertips. Evie pressed her hand to her mouth, her eyes pressed tightly shut. She couldn't wait any longer.

"What do you mean I can't see him?"

Celine cupped Evie's elbow in her hand and walked her the length of the corridor. The lawyer was in a hurry, heading toward the jail. "He'd rather not."

"I want to talk to him."

"Evie, please. I'm his lawyer—"

"And I love him."

The two women eyed each other a long moment.

A door opened. The bailiff brought Cole into the hall.

"I have one thing to say to you," Evie announced from the other side of Celine.

Cole stared at the floor.

She hated him for doing this alone. She loved him beyond all reason. If he couldn't deal with that, so be it. "You said I was a fool for loving a man blindly. Are all those people fools? Because they love you too. Bud, your aunt, your friends."

"Where were they when I needed them?" he asked, allowing himself one brief moment of bitterness for all the years he and his mother had suffered.

"Maybe they were there all along. Trying to help you. Like I am." She stepped toward him, her legs shaking, her fingernails digging into her palms. "Maybe you drove them away—the way you're doing with me. You wouldn't confide in anyone, let anyone in. It's what your mother did, keeping up appearances, protecting the family. You learned it from her. That this was shameful. That it was you and her versus your father. You *learned* not to turn to anyone."

He turned his face.

She clutched his arm. The words emerged brokenly, her voice failing. "Let me love you. Please."

He hesitated. A vein beat in his jaw. He opened his mouth.

The door opened on the long antiseptic hall that led back to the jail. He looked down it. Then he looked at her. A choice he couldn't make. The bailiff tugged his arm.

He left.

Evie heard doors clang shut all the way down the hall.

Celine touched her hand. "Maybe he has to do this alone."

"He doesn't *have* to," Evie snapped. The tears broke free. "No one *has* to go through this alone."

"It's all he ever saw."

But what about her? Had he stopped seeing her?

Evie covered her mouth with her hand. It was selfish. It was all she had. She ached for him, and he loved her too much to let her share his pain.

"I've spoken with the people's representative, with the defense, and have come to the conclusion that there is not enough evidence to link Mr. Raynes's death to the assault his son committed on him. As for the other charges, they've lapsed under the statute of limitations. The defendant is hereby released." The gavel banged down.

Evie held her breath. Cole showed no emotion whatsoever. She didn't know whether to cheer or cry. They'd won. But how much else had they lost?

Vivian grasped her in a hug, shoving a tissue into her hand. Bud did the same. She tried to smile. She longed to break away, to see him before he left.

"What's the matter?" Vivian asked. "Aren't you happy?"

"I need some time. I guess I need to be alone a minute." She laughed at the irony. At last she understood the need to retreat into one's shell, to barricade oneself against the world. She wanted to tell Cole that. He was moving toward the side door, shaking hands with the bailiff.

Evie pushed through the crowd of departing spectators, accepting their handshakes, their smiles. She'd called on all of them, his friends, his co-workers. Her first instinct had been to gather support in a time of trouble.

Cole had handled his troubles alone. Could he ever learn to share them?

She reached the railing at last, stretching across it to congratulate Celine. They shared a hug, then the lawyer leaned back, noting the direction of Evie's gaze. "He should be out in an hour. Paperwork."

Evie nodded. She wasn't sure where she'd be.

The corridor was empty save for the occasional court employee walking from office to office. Evie waited for Cole. She couldn't wait forever. She knew she had to be ready, in case he told her one more time that he wanted her out of his life. She'd done everything she could to convince him that love was worth fighting for. Real love. The kind that put the other person first without losing sight of one's own needs.

And, like any other battle, sometimes the fight was lost. She had to be realistic. They'd had a week together and three days apart. It wasn't enough to build a relationship on. Unless love was enough.

A man had to accept that love could be everything.

A woman had to risk telling him that.

He came around the corner. He stopped when he saw her.

She stood taller. She'd been twirling his cowboy hat over and over in her hands. She hefted it nervously, her voice a touch high. "I got used to seeing men wearing these everywhere around here. Thought you might want it."

He looked at her a long moment, the hardness in his eyes covering up something else. Sorrow? Longing?

She couldn't say it for him. She had to wait, to listen, to be ready whether the news was good or bad.

In sickness or in health, she thought.

She extended the hat.

He edged forward and took it, looking down as he spun it once on his hand.

"I asked everyone to wait outside," she said. "They're all here to congratulate you. To welcome you home."

He looked up.

"To Montana."

"Mm."

"Think you'll stay here?"

"I've got a job back in Michigan. If Bud'll have me."

"You're his star mechanic; of course he'll have you." She paused. "So will I."

A secretary's high heels clicked down the hall. Cole waited until she'd passed. Evie leaned toward him.

He raked the hall with a gaze. "Shall we go?"

Her heart fell. So that was it. He wanted to join the others. He didn't want to be alone with her. She should have known. He'd all but said it.

She walked toward the door.

He touched her arm as she passed him, spinning her softly toward him. "I never got a chance to thank you."

Past tense? She tried to lift her shoulders in a shrug.

He had no words for this either. He stepped forward. "I'm sorry."

"Don't be. I—"

"Shh." His kiss was rough, tender, desperate, thankful.

She clung to him, unable to breathe, to hope.

He balanced his forehead to hers, their noses just touching. "You stuck by me," he said.

She peeked up. Flecks of light glinted in his eyes. A smile's creases were etched into his temples. He looked tired. And wonderful.

She squeezed him until she couldn't breathe and didn't care. "I couldn't leave," she said. "I knew you didn't want me here, but what was I supposed to do? Turn tail at the first sign of trouble?"

"Run away?"

She gripped his shirt. It was long past time he forgave himself for saving his own life. "You did the best you could. You survived. Maybe you'd handle it differently now, but you didn't do anything wrong then."

"You didn't listen to me."

"I listened. I just didn't obey."

"Is that what it's all about? Love, honor, obey?"

"Only if the man you love makes sense. There should be a footnote on every marriage license."

"A consumer warning."

"Yeah." She smeared a tear off her cheek.

"Yeah." He kissed her forehead.

"What are you grinning at?" she demanded.

"You. You saved my life. You won't let anything stop you when you're right."

"Including you."

Her body tucked against his, he nuzzled her hair, his lips skimming her forehead.

Her lungs filled with his familiar musky scent. The tears welled.

"I'm sorry I pushed you away," he whispered.

"So am I." She tossed her hair and looked up at him, sniffing loudly. She pounded a soft fist against his chest. "You think I like you telling me to get lost? It hurt like hell, Creek. But I understood. It's about time somebody did."

Cole looked into her gleaming eyes. He marveled at this love stuff, the way it stripped a man of all his timeworn defenses, cutting through every protective barrier. She saw through him, past everything to his faults and fears.

She'd taken on the courts, the police, the lawyers. She'd taken him on when he'd stopped believing in himself, in love.

Apparently, the woman had her own doubts. She worried a button on his shirt until he picked up the hint. "What is it now?"

"We've only had a week together."

"Not much to build a relationship on."

"No."

"We had a little longer than that."

"What do you mean?"

He tipped her chin up. "I loved you the minute I saw you."

"You did?"

"Head over heels."

"You never told me."

"There's a lot I never told you."

She gazed up at him, freckles wet, lashes clumped like the rays of a star.

"I know you love me," he said. "I know you'll stand up for me when I deserve it and chew me out when I don't. That's real love, Evie."

"That's being a woman."

"Damn straight."

He kissed her again, eagerly this time. He didn't care who came through the hall.

"Time to go?" she asked. Minutes had passed. They stood swaying in each other's arms.

He took a deep breath. "Time to take on the world."

"They tried to help."

"I know."

Arm in arm, they strolled toward the door. He pushed it open. There was no one there.

Evie put her hand on her hip. "I can't believe they didn't wait!"

Cole settled the cowboy hat on his head, a knowing squint in his eyes. "Guess they got tired."

"Of course, it took them forever to release you. I was afraid—" She blushed. "Actually, I was about to start a sit-in to protest. Or at the very least get up a petition."

"You would."

"What was the holdup?"

"I had to talk to the judge."

"More red tape?"

"Marriage license."

She blinked very slowly.

"Might as well make this legal," he said. "It's all about commitment, right?"

"Cole."

He pulled her to his side. "No more running away, Evie. I want to make this permanent."

She threw her arms around his neck so hard, she practically knocked him over.

"Hey!"

She kissed him, his lips, his cheek, his neck.

He laughed and set her on her feet. "Whoa there. I think we'll find everyone at the restaurant down the street. Rehearsal dinner."

Evie wasn't moving. "I'm happy right here," she murmured, her head tucked against his shoulder.

He felt a familiar heat. "We'll have to stick around for blood tests. Then we can finish our drive."

"You want to continue?"

"Might make a nice honeymoon. Seattle, Oregon, the Napa Valley. New Orleans eventually. We've got a lot of ground to cover in that little car."

"And a lifetime to do it."

He kissed her one last time. "Where is your car?"

"Other side of the building."

They walked back inside, down the long corridors past offices and cubicles. At the back door a security guard sat at a table. He nodded to them as they walked outside into the sunshine. Evie oohed and ahhed at the crystalline beauty of the mountains. Cole looked at nothing but her.

The guard turned his radio up.

"*This is* Austin in the Evening. *It's seven o'clock Carolina time, four o'clock on the coast.*" And five P.M., one hour from quitting time, in Montana. The guard sipped his cup of coffee. This was one of his favorite shows.

"Do you believe in psychics?" the radio host asked. "If so, Fiona Alexander, one of the nation's top psychics, is with us again tonight by popular demand. Evenin', Fiona."

"Thank you, Austin."

"I see the phones are lit up already. Before we get to that, you had something to share with us?"

"You know, people always ask about the results of my insight. What happened to a particular caller? Did she find her soul mate?"

"We've heard back from more than a few. You've almost made me a believer."

"It's about time. However, tonight, before we get started, I'd like to send a message to a woman who called the week before last. Eve, your search is ended. But you know, as I do, that your real journey is just beginning. Happy trails, my dear."

EPILOGUE

"A minivan." Cole settled his hands on his hips. Circling the behemoth in the garage parking lot in Dearborn, he squinted doubtfully at his wife. "A Harley, I could see. A Mercedes convertible. A Corvette, sixty-five, black split-window coupe—"

"It's the latest in minivan design," Evie insisted. "Perfect for growing families."

"It's suburbia on wheels."

"Get in, Creek."

Bud slapped him on the back. "Quit your whining."

"You going to have any trouble keeping up?" Cole asked his former boss.

"Ha! I'm retired six months, and you think I don't remember how to change a tire?"

"With your back you're not changing any tires," Vivian called from the office. "That's Billy's job."

The teenager Cole had hired to help with the basics glanced up from the tune-up he was working on. He hated being called Billy. "It's Bill," he yelled.

The day before, the former runaway had asked Cole who these old people were anyway.

"They're family," Cole had said. He'd meant every word.

At the moment his more immediate family waited impatiently. "I swear, he's worse than Bud," Evie said to Vivian, loud enough for everyone to hear. "Can't tear him away from this place. This'll be our first vacation in two years."

"Don't you worry about a thing," Bud assured him. "I'll fix everything you've done wrong to the place since I retired."

"I know you will," Cole muttered. He gave Bud a hug, made sure Vivian's lasted twice as long, then sauntered to the driver's side of the minivan.

Evie had already marked the seat with her sun hat.

"You mean I don't even get to drive?" he groused.

"Shoo. I'm doing the first leg." She swatted him on the behind.

He looped an arm around her waist and gave her a lingering kiss. "Okay. I'll let you drive."

"Let?"

"Daddy, let's go."

He chuckled at Evie's outrage and his daughter's imperious whine. Their three-year-old fidgeted in the backseat.

"Am I safe?" the tiny dynamo demanded.

He leaned in and checked the straps on her child safety seat. Evie wouldn't have bought it if it hadn't been the safest product on the market. Emily wouldn't let the car start unless her daddy checked it out himself.

"You're safe, sunshine."

"And Kelly?" Evie asked. Harried and hurried, she reviewed her list of things to take.

Cole checked the safety seat for their twelve-month-old son. "Snug as a bug in a rug."

Emily squealed in delight. He kissed her on the ear and made her laugh again. "You watch your brother now."

"I will."

"Will you kiss Mommy again?" she asked.

"In a minute."

Apparently Mrs. Creek had different ideas. She was peering at a map. "I think we can make Albany by tonight and Maine by tomorrow. That is, if we don't spend too much time in Vermont."

He took the map out of her hands. "We'll get there when we get there. We've got three weeks, Evie."

She looked up at him, focusing at last on him and him only. She sighed. "Five years."

"Five years ago today. Happy anniversary." He kissed her long and slow.

"You'll never get going at this rate," Bud called.

Vivian shushed him.

"Five years," Evie murmured, her cheek grazing the side of his.

"And all you can buy me is a minivan."

She huffed at his teasing. "It's only a test-drive. It's the latest in minivan design. Someone's got to check it out."

"Got your notebooks?"

"About ten of them."

"Still love me?"

"I don't have to keep notes on that. I haven't found anything I'd change about you."

"Can't improve on perfection."

"Nope."

He kissed her hair, hugging her hard and long. "I love you, Evie."

"I love you."

"Remember that old Conquest?"

She defended their family sedan. "It's held up very well."

"Now you've got me into minivans."

She planted a sassy kiss on his cheek. "There's a lot more I'd like to get you in."

"Mm. Water beds? Whirlpools?"

"Forget the maps. Just find me a hotel with baby-sitting services."

He scowled. "You'd better check 'em out. I don't want just anybody watching these kids."

Evie laughed and pulled a notebook from her over-sized shoulder bag. "I have recommendations from coast to coast."

"Then let's hit the road."

She hopped in the van. That first step seemed a little high. She made a note.

Cole got in on the passenger side. She watched him while he checked on the kids once more. She wasn't surprised he'd turned out to be a loving father. He had infinite patience, a voice he never raised, and the security to let his children take risks.

At the moment theirs were baby-step risks, the chances adventurous toddlers took. Evie, with her encyclopedic knowledge of dangerous products, wasn't half so sanguine about the mischief Emily and Kelly got into.

It didn't matter. Between the two of them, she and Cole had made two wonderful little people. They'd also made a marriage that grew and deepened every day. She thought back to the fears that had dogged her in earlier days. She couldn't imagine not being able to talk to Cole now, sharing every fear, every worry. And he was the same.

"You going to sit or you going to drive?"

She'd been staring across the car at him. "Just remembering."

He leaned over. They met in the middle for a kiss. "Put it in gear, babe. Let's see what this pile of metal can do."

She spared a glance at the backseat. "You know, those seats all fold down." She waggled her brows.

He barked a laugh and pulled his cowboy hat low on his forehead. She didn't miss the sly smile that stayed on his face. He glanced over, put his seat belt on, and settled in for the ride. "Wake me when we get to Albany."

"You're going to sleep?" she said with a huff.

"I trust your driving. Besides, I get the feeling we're going to stay up late tonight."

Tiny thrills of fire raced beneath her skin. She grinned. "Promises, promises."

"You got it. The forever kind."

She glanced in the rearview mirror and pulled out of the lot. Their journey was just starting.

THE EDITORS' CORNER

The four new LOVESWEPTs headed your way next month boast the sexiest season's greetings you'll ever read. While the chestnuts are roasting, be sure to treat yourself with romances guaranteed to put the sizzle in your holidays.

Marcia Evanick charms our socks off again with **MY TRUE LOVE GAVE TO ME**, LOVESWEPT #770. When she awakens Christmas morning, Megan Lemaine gazes, astonished, at the pear tree—with a partridge—in her backyard! Then Tate Brady comes courting, seducing her senses with fiery kisses while a dozen days of enchantment fill her with wonder. With this funny, touching, and utterly irresistible tale of love as magical as a Christmas miracle, Marcia Evanick creates a romance to cherish for always!

BORN TO BE WILD, LOVESWEPT #771, is

the next smoldering novel in Donna Kauffman's <u>The Three Musketeers</u> trilogy. Zach Brogan is sexier than sin, a globe-trotting wild man whose bad boy smile beckons Dana Colburne to taste thrills only he can deliver! He'd always sensed the secret wildness that burned inside his childhood pal, had tempted her into trouble more than once, but now he wants the woman she's become to feel his fire. Untamable, outrageous, explosively sexy, Donna Kauffman's heroes like dancing on the edge and women who don't make it easy—but no one sizzles hotter than guys who act bad to the bone but are oh-so-good!

Romantic Times award winner Laura Taylor explores the darkest shadows in the human heart with **SEDUCED**, LOVESWEPT #772. He'd loved Maggie Holden for as long as he could remember, had ached as she wed another, but now Noah Sutton wants to make the hauntingly beautiful widow his at last! Tainted by a tragic betrayal, her innocence destroyed, Maggie has retreated from the world. Noah stuns her with passion, igniting a soul-deep longing to be cherished—and to be believed. Rich with poignant emotion, thrilling in their intensity, Laura Taylor's novels celebrate the healing power of hope.

Bonnie Pega sets pulses pounding in **THE REBEL AND HIS BRIDE**, LOVESWEPT #773. Annabelle Pace was Gregory Talbot's true love, until she left him with no explanation. Now the beautiful seductress is back in town, and he is determined to get answers, if he can keep his hands off her delectable body long enough. Annabelle refuses to play second fiddle to the minister's causes, but with one kiss, he unleashes all her pent-up desires and recaptures her soul. Brimming with desire, Bonnie Pega offers a novel of passion too fierce to be denied.

Happy reading!

With warmest wishes,

Beth de Guzman

Shauna Summers

Beth de Guzman   Shauna Summers

Senior Editor   Associate Editor

P.S. Watch for these Bantam women's fiction titles coming in January: From Jane Feather—the incomparable author of the national bestsellers VIOLET and VALENTINE—comes **VANITY,** her newest unforgettable romance. **BREAKFAST IN BED,** a classic romance by *New York Times* bestselling author Sandra Brown, will be available in hardcover. In **DEATH ELIGIBLE** Judith Henry Wall sets out to discover how far one family will go to protect itself—when one of them is guilty of murder. Tamara Leigh, author of PAGAN BRIDE, presents **SAXON BRIDE,** the story of a fiercely handsome warrior and the breathtakingly lovely woman who leaves him torn between his duty and an agonizing truth. And finally, **NIGHT SINS,** the acclaimed national bestseller from Tami Hoag, will be out in paperback. Be sure to see next month's LOVESWEPTs for a preview of these remarkable novels. And immediately following this page, preview the Bantam women's fiction titles on sale *now*!

Don't miss these extraordinary books
by your favorite Bantam authors

On sale in November:

AMANDA
by Kay Hooper

HEAVEN'S PRICE
by Sandra Brown

MASTER
OF PARADISE
by Katherine O'Neal

TEXAS OUTLAW
by Adrienne deWolfe

When was the last time a novel seduced you?

*With her spellbinding imagination and seductive voice,
Kay Hooper is the only author worthy of being called
today's successor to Victoria Holt. Now this powerful
storyteller has created a unique and stunning tale of contemporary suspense that begins with a mysterious homecoming and ends in a shattering explosion of passion,
greed, and murder. And all because a stranger says her
name is . . .*

AMANDA
by Kay Hooper

July, 1975

Thunder rolled and boomed, echoing the way it did
when a storm came over the mountains on a hot
night, and the wind-driven rain lashed the trees and
furiously pelted the windowpanes of the big house.
The nine-year-old girl shivered, her cotton night-
gown soaked and clinging to her, and her slight body
was stiff as she stood in the center of the dark bedroom.

"Mama—"

"Shhhh! Don't, baby, don't make any noise. Just
stand there, very still, and wait for me."

They called her baby often, her mother, her father, because she'd been so difficult to conceive and
was so cherished once they had her. So beloved. That
was why they had named her Amanda, her father had

explained, lifting her up to ride upon his broad shoulders, because she was so perfect and so worthy of their love.

She didn't feel perfect now. She felt cold and emptied out and dreadfully afraid. And the sound of her mother's voice, so thin and desperate, frightened Amanda even more. The bottom had fallen out of her world so suddenly that she was still numbly bewildered and broken, and her big gray eyes followed her mother with the piteous dread of one who had lost everything except a last fragile, unspeakably precious tie to what had been.

Whispering between rumbles of thunder, she asked, "Mama, where will we go?"

"Away, far away, baby." The only illumination in the bedroom was provided by angry nature as lightning split the stormy sky outside, and Christine Daulton used the flashes to guide her in stuffing clothes into an old canvas duffel bag. She dared not turn on any lights, and the need to hurry was so fierce it nearly strangled her.

She hadn't room for them, but she pushed her journals into the bag as well because she had to have *something* of this place to take with her, and something of her life with Brian. *Oh, dear God, Brian . . .* She raked a handful of jewelry from the box on the dresser, tasting blood because she was biting her bottom lip to keep herself from screaming. There was no time, no time, she had to get Amanda away from here.

"Wait here," she told her daughter.

"No! Mama, please—"

"Shhhh! All right, Amanda, come with me—but you have to be quiet." Moments later, down the hall in her daughter's room, Christine fumbled for more clothing and thrust it into the bulging bag. She helped the silent, trembling girl into dry clothing, faded jeans and a tee shirt. "Shoes?"

Amanda found a pair of dirty sneakers and shoved her feet into them. Her mother grasped her hand and led her from the room, both of them consciously tiptoeing. Then, at the head of the stairs, Amanda suddenly let out a moan of anguish and tried to pull her hand free. "Oh, I *can't*—"

"Shhhh," Christine warned urgently. "Amanda—"

Even whispering, Amanda's voice held a desperate intensity. "Mama, please, Mama, I have to get something—I can't leave it here, please, Mama—it'll only take a second—"

She had no idea what could be so precious to her daughter, but Christine wasn't about to drag her down the stairs in this state of wild agitation. The child was already in shock, a breath away from absolute hysteria. "All right, but hurry. And *be quiet.*"

As swift and silent as a shadow, Amanda darted back down the hallway and vanished into her bedroom. She reappeared less than a minute later, shoving something into the front pocket of her jeans. Christine didn't pause to find out what was so important that Amanda couldn't bear to leave it behind; she simply grabbed her daughter's free hand and continued down the stairs.

The grandfather clock on the landing whirred and bonged a moment before they reached it, announcing in sonorous tones that it was two A.M. The sound was too familiar to startle either of them, and they hurried on without pause. The front door was still open, as they'd left it, and Christine didn't bother to pull it shut behind them as they went through to the wide porch.

The wind had blown rain halfway over the porch to the door, and Amanda dimly heard her shoes squeak on the wet stone. Then she ducked her head against the rain and stuck close to her mother as they raced for the car parked several yards away. By the time she was sitting in the front seat watching her mother fumble with the keys, Amanda was soaked again and shivering, despite a temperature in the seventies.

The car's engine coughed to life, and its headlights stabbed through the darkness and sheeting rain to illuminate the graveled driveway. Amanda turned her head to the side as the car jolted toward the paved road, and she caught her breath when she saw a light bobbing far away between the house and the stables, as if someone was running with a flashlight. Running toward the car that, even then, turned onto the paved road and picked up speed as it left the house behind.

Quickly, Amanda turned her gaze forward again, rubbing her cold hands together, swallowing hard as sickness rose in her aching throat. "Mama? We can't come back, can we? We can't ever come back?"

The tears running down her ashen cheeks almost but not quite blinding her, Christine Daulton replied, "No, Amanda. We can't ever come back."

HEAVEN'S PRICE

by Sandra Brown

AVAILABLE
IN PAPERBACK

"One of romance fiction's brightest stars."
—*Dallas Morning News*

With one huge bestseller after another, Sandra Brown has earned a place among America's most popular romance writers. Now the New York Times bestselling author of TEMPERATURES RISING brings us this classic, sensuous novel filled with her trademark blend of humor and passion, about a woman who thought she knew her destiny until she learns that fate—and her heart—have something else in store.

From the award-winning author of PRINCESS OF
THIEVES

MASTER OF PARADISE
by Katherine O'Neal

*As the privateer bore down on her ship, Gabrielle Ashton-
Cross recognized all too well the magnificent, leonine figure
at its prow. Once she had resisted his arrogant passion, had
survived his betrayal to become the toast of London. And
even now she might escape him, for her sword was like
lightning. Yet the moment their gazes locked across the
rolling deck, she knew that Rodrigo Soro had every intention of taming her to his will at last. Gabrielle hadn't
journeyed so far from home to fulfill a lifelong dream only
to surrender to a pirate king. But this time when he took
her in his arms, would she have the strength to fight the
only man who could ever promise her paradise?*

"*Ella â minga,*" Rodrigo had told his men. *She's mine.*

He was so confident, so secure. Yet there were
some things even his carefully placed spies couldn't
know. Things that had long ago closed the door on
any future with Rodrigo—even if he hadn't thrown
his life away to become the bloodiest pirate of the
seven seas.

Gabrielle thought of that night, eight long years
ago, when they'd said their farewells. She'd seen the
proof back then of his dark passions, of the menacing

sensuality of the inner self he'd hidden from an unsuspecting world. Of the cold, ruthless way he could pursue his goals. Hadn't she learned that night to pursue her own aims just as coldly, just as ruthlessly? But she'd never seen this anger, this impression of raw, unrestricted violence that sparked the air between them. It scared her suddenly, as she realized for the first time where she was—alone in a locked room with the one man who was truly dangerous to her designs. With her ripped skirts up about her hips. With him pressing his all-too-persuasive body into the softly yielding flesh of her own. With an erection fueled by years of frustrated desires.

As if reading her thoughts, he softened his tone. Still holding her head in his hands, he said, "But that's over. We're together now. I've come here to rescue you."

She put her hands to his shoulders and pushed him away. "Just what is it you're rescuing me *from*?"

"From the clutches of England, of course."

She couldn't believe what she was hearing. "I rescued *myself* from England, thank you very much! Did you imagine I'd wait all this time, like some damsel in distress, for you to fashion a miracle and rescue me? When I had no indication that you ever thought about me at all?"

His hand stilled in the act of reaching for her breast. "I thought about you always. I never stopped longing for you."

"You never sent me word. Was I supposed to read your mind? Wait for a man who walked out of my life without so much as a backward glance? Without regrets of any kind?"

"You're wrong, Gabé. I regretted very much having to leave you behind."

"You *regret*? You knew what you were going to do and you didn't tell me. I can't believe the arrogance of you thinking you could waltz back into my life and dictate my future after all you did to me."

His hand made the arrested journey and slid over her breast. "Is a future with me so formidable a prospect?" he asked in a husky tone.

She shoved him away and fought to sit up. "Future? What kind of life would I have with you? A pirate's wench? Hunted by the law? Hung by the neck till I'm dead? You don't seem to understand, Rodrigo. You stand in the way of all I hold dear. You once told me I didn't fit into your plans. Well, now you don't fit into mine."

"You have no feelings for me at all, I suppose?"

She lifted her head defiantly and said, "None!"

He took her wrists and wrenched her up from the bed so she came crashing against his chest. The blow was like colliding with a brick wall. "I *know* you. I know the passions of your soul. It matters not what you say. You're mine now. This time I surrender you to no man. I made a mistake with you once before. But that," he added bitterly, "is a blunder I won't make again."

You're mine now. Staking his claim. Taking possession of her like a bauble he fancied. As if she had no feelings. Permitting her no say at all.

"I shan't let you do this," she vowed. "Your men already tried to take me against my will. Do you think I'd fight them off, only to let another pirate succeed where they failed?"

He was insulted, as she'd intended. She could see it in the tightening of his jaw, in the ferocious flare of his lion's eyes. She pulled away, but he followed, pushing her back to his bunk as he stepped toward her with stormy eyes. As she backed away across the expanse of red silk, she came up sharply against the wall—the one with the collection of weapons within handy reach.

He caught the flash of the blade as she snatched it from the wall. Incensed, he grabbed her arm and yanked her to her feet. But he didn't know what an expert swordswoman she'd become. Determined to fight him, she swung the sword around and put the cutting edge to his throat.

TEXAS OUTLAW

by Adrienne deWolfe

For a lady train robber, seduction was a game—until a handsome lawman changed the rules. . . .

In this sneak peek, Fancy Holleday has only a few minutes to dispose of Marshal Rawlins before her band of outlaws boards the train. And desperation drives her to a reckless act.

"Marshal!" Fancy's bellow rattled the windows and caused at least one passenger to douse his lap with turtle soup. "Arrest this man!"

"You want the preacher cuffed, eh?"

"Yes, sir, I most certainly do!"

"What in blazes for?"

Fancy hiked her chin. Obviously, Mama Rawlins had neglected to teach her son the finer points of etiquette.

"Because that . . . that *beast* of a man dared to . . ." She paused dramatically. "To grope me!"

Rawlins chuckled, a rich, warm sound in the breathless silence of the car. "Whoa, darlin'. No one was over there groping anything that you didn't give away a good long time ago."

She bristled. He had seen through her ruse! Despite her stylish emerald traveling suit and the demure black ringlets that framed her face, Cord

Rawlins had pegged her for a trollop. She wasn't sure she could ever forgive him for that.

"If you're not man enough to defend my honor," she said coolly, "then I shall be happy to speak to the railroad detective whom I saw dining here earlier."

Every eye in the car shifted eagerly back to Rawlins. He appeared undaunted. Hooking his thumbs over his gunbelt, he strolled to her side. She was surprised when she realized he was only about three inches taller than she. Standing in the doorway, he had appeared much larger. Nevertheless, the lawman exuded an aura of command.

"Well, preacher?" Rawlins tipped his Stetson back with a forefinger. A curl so dark brown that it verged on black tumbled across the untanned peak of his forehead. "Speak your piece."

The cleric continued to gape. "Well, I, um . . ."

"Spit it out, man. Did you or did you not grope this . . ." Rawlins paused, arching a brow at the straining buttons of Fancy's bodice. ". . . this, er, lady."

She glared into his dancing eyes, then let her gaze travel down his face. The man had dimples. Bottomless dimples. They looked like two sickle moons attached to the dazzling white of his grin. She thought there should be a law somewhere against virile Texicans with heart-stopping smiles. Cord Rawlins had probably left dozens of calf-eyed sweethearts sighing for him back home on the range.

"I'm sure there must be some reasonable explanation," the preacher meanwhile babbled. His scarecrow body trembled as he towered over Rawlins. "I'm sure the young lady just made a mistake—"

"The only mistake I made," Fancy interrupted, "was thinking that this lawman might come to the defense of a lady. No doubt Marshal Rawlins finds such courtesies an imposition on his authority."

"Begging your pardon, ma'am." He indulged her this time with a roguish wink. "I thought you did a mighty fine job of defending yourself."

Oh, did you now? She seethed. *Then just wait 'til you get a load of my .32!* If only that blessed moment would come. Where in hell was Diego?

"Show's over, folks." Rawlins waved his audience back to their meals. "Your pigeons are getting cold."

"That's it?" She gaped. "That's all you're going to do to help me?"

" 'Fraid so, ma'am. You aren't any the worse for wear, as far as I can see. And I reckon Parson Brown isn't any worse off, either."

"Why, you—!" Fancy remembered just in time that ladies didn't curse. "You can't just walk away," she insisted, grabbing Rawlins's sleeve and hoping he would mistake her panic for indignation.

"Says who?"

A nerve-rending screech suddenly pierced the expectancy in the car. Fancy had a heartbeat to identify the braking of iron wheels; in the next instant, the floorboards heaved, throwing her against Rawlins's chest. Silver, crystal, and a diner's toupee flew; she cringed to hear the other passengers scream as she clung to her savior's neck. Rawlins's curse ended in an "umph." Fancy was grateful when he sacrificed his own spine rather than let hers smash from the table to the carpet. For a moment, Rawlins's tobacco, leather, and muscled body imprinted themselves on her senses. Then her mind whirred back into action. She had to get his Colt.

Having made a career of outsmarting men, Fancy found it no great feat to shriek, thrash, and wail in a parody of feminine terror. She wriggled across Rawlins's hips and succeeded in hooking her heel behind his knee. She knew she could pin him for only a moment, but a moment was all she needed to slip her Smith & Wesson from her boot—and jam its muzzle into his groin.

"Whoa, darling," she taunted above the distant sounds of gunfire.

His face turned scarlet, and she knew he had assessed his situation. He couldn't reach his holster without first dumping her to the floor. And that would be risky, she gloated silently. Most risky indeed.

"Have you lost your goddamned mind?"

"My dear marshal, you really must learn to be more respectful of ladies," she retorted above the other passengers' groans. "Now real slowly, I want you to raise your hands and put them behind your head."

On sale in December:

BREAKFAST IN BED
by Sandra Brown

NIGHT SINS
by Tami Hoag
available in paperback

VANITY
by Jane Feather

DEATH ELIGIBLE
by Judith Henry Wall

SAXON BRIDE
by Tamara Leigh

To enter the sweepstakes outlined below, you must respond by the date specified and follow all entry instructions published elsewhere in this offer.

DREAM COME TRUE SWEEPSTAKES

Sweepstakes begins 9/1/94, ends 1/15/96. To qualify for the Early Bird Prize, entry must be received by the date specified elsewhere in this offer. Winners will be selected in random drawings on 2/29/96 by an independent judging organization whose decisions are final. Early Bird winner will be selected in a separate drawing from among all qualifying entries.

Odds of winning determined by total number of entries received. Distribution not to exceed 300 million.

Estimated maximum retail value of prizes: Grand (1) $25,000 (cash alternative $20,000); First (1) $2,000; Second (1) $750; Third (50) $75; Fourth (1,000) $50; Early Bird (1) $5,000. Total prize value: $86,500.

Automobile and travel trailer must be picked up at a local dealer; all other merchandise prizes will be shipped to winners. Awarding of any prize to a minor will require written permission of parent/guardian. If a trip prize is won by a minor, s/he must be accompanied by parent/legal guardian. Trip prizes subject to availability and must be completed within 12 months of date awarded. Blackout dates may apply. Early Bird trip is on a space available basis and does not include port charges, gratuities, optional shore excursions and onboard personal purchases. Prizes are not transferable or redeemable for cash except as specified. No substitution for prizes except as necessary due to unavailability. Travel trailer and/or automobile license and registration fees are winners' responsibility as are any other incidental expenses not specified herein.

Early Bird Prize may not be offered in some presentations of this sweepstakes. Grand through third prize winners will have the option of selecting any prize offered at level won. All prizes will be awarded. Drawing will be held at 204 Center Square Road, Bridgeport, NJ 08014. Winners need not be present. For winners list (available in June, 1996), send a self-addressed, stamped envelope by 1/15/96 to: Dream Come True Winners, P.O. Box 572, Gibbstown, NJ 08027.

THE FOLLOWING APPLIES TO THE SWEEPSTAKES ABOVE:

No purchase necessary. No photocopied or mechanically reproduced entries will be accepted. Not responsible for lost, late, misdirected, damaged, incomplete, illegible, or postage-die mail. Entries become the property of sponsors and will not be returned.

Winner(s) will be notified by mail. Winner(s) may be required to sign and return an affidavit of eligibility/release within 14 days of date on notification or an alternate may be selected. Except where prohibited by law, entry constitutes permission to use of winners' names, hometowns, and likenesses for publicity without additional compensation. Void where prohibited or restricted. All federal, state, provincial, and local laws and regulations apply.

All prize values are in U.S. currency. Presentation of prizes may vary; values at a given prize level will be approximately the same. All taxes are winners' responsibility.

Canadian residents, in order to win, must first correctly answer a time-limited skill testing question administered by mail. Any litigation regarding the conduct and awarding of a prize in this publicity contest by a resident of the province of Quebec may be submitted to the Regie des loteries et courses du Quebec.

Sweepstakes is open to legal residents of the U.S., Canada, and Europe (in those areas where made available) who have received this offer.

Sweepstakes in sponsored by Ventura Associates, 1211 Avenue of the Americas, New York, NY 10036 and presented by independent businesses. Employees of these, their advertising agencies and promotional companies involved in this promotion, and their immediate families, agents, successors, and assignees shall be ineligible to participate in the promotion and shall not be eligible for any prizes covered herein.   SWP 3/95

DON'T MISS THESE FABULOUS
BANTAM WOMEN'S FICTION TITLES

On Sale in November

AMANDA *by bestselling author* Kay Hooper
*"Don't miss a story that will keep your reading light on until
well into the night."*—Catherine Coulter

With her spellbinding imagination and seductive voice, Kay Hooper is the
only author worthy of being called today's successor to Victoria Holt. Now
this powerful storyteller has created a stunning tale of contemporary suspense that begins with a mysterious homecoming and ends in a shattering
explosion of passion, greed, and murder.____ 09957-4 $19.95/$24.95 in Canada

MASTER OF PARADISE *by* Katherine O'Neal
Winner of *Romantic Times*' Best Sensual Historical Romance
Award for THE LAST HIGHWAYMAN
*"Katherine O'Neal is the queen of romantic adventure,
reigning over a court of intrigue, sensuality, and good
old-fashioned storytelling."*—Affaire de Coeur

Katherine O'Neal unveils a spectacular new novel of romantic adventure—
a tantalizing tale of a notorious pirate, a rebellious beauty, and a dangerously erotic duel of hearts.   ____ 56956-2 $5.50/$7.99

TEXAS OUTLAW *by sparkling new talent* Adrienne deWolfe
Combining the delightful wit of Arnette Lamb and the tender emotion of
Pamela Morsi, this spectacular historical romance is a dazzling debut from
an author destined to be a star.   ____ 57395-0 $4.99/$6.99

New York Times bestselling author Sandra Brown's
HEAVEN'S PRICE
Now available in paperback   ____ 57157-5 $5.50/$6.99

Ask for these books at your local bookstore or use this page to order.

Please send me the books I have checked above. I am enclosing $____ (add $2.50 to
cover postage and handling). Send check or money order, no cash or C.O.D.'s, please.

Name _____

Address _____

City/State/Zip _____

Send order to: Bantam Books, Dept. FN159, 2451 S. Wolf Rd., Des Plaines, IL 60018
Allow four to six weeks for delivery.

Prices and availability subject to change without notice.   FN 159 11/95